Dear Reader

I went to a friend's wedding recently, and was touched deeply by the ceremony, by the exchange of vows, by the circle of warmth encapsulating the bride and groom.

I felt how being near those totally and utterly in love has a lasting impact on all of those who share that moment.

I wanted to write about the women behind the scenes, the ones who make those special days happen, the ones who play fairy godmother, helping to create a memory built on love that extends beyond the span of days, months and years. The ones who, no matter how expert they are at helping others, can't quite sort out their own lives.

I hope you enjoy reading their stories as much as I enjoyed writing them. Look out for *The Best Man's Baby* and *A Convenient Groom*, coming soon in Tender Romance™!

Best Wishes,

Darcy Maguire wanted to grow up to be a fairy, but her wings never grew, her magic never worked and her life was no fairytale. But one thing she knew for certain was that she was going to find her soul-mate and live happily ever after. Darcy found her dark and handsome hero on a blind date, married him a year later, and found that love truly is the soul of creativity. With four children too young to play matchmaker for (yet!), Darcy satisfies the romantic in her by finding true love for her fictional characters. It was this passion for romance, and her ability to sit still every day, that led to the publication of her first novel, HER MARRIAGE SECRET. Darcy lives in Melbourne, Australia, and loves to read widely, sew and sneak off to the movies without the kids.

Recent titles by the same author:

ALMOST MARRIED
ACCIDENTAL BRIDE
HER MARRIAGE SECRET

A PROFESSIONAL ENGAGEMENT

BY
DARCY MAGUIRE

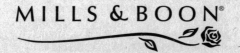

MILLS & BOON®

First published in Great Britain 2004
Harlequin Mills & Boon Limited,
Eton House, 18-24 Paradise Road, Richmond, Surrey TW9 1SR

© Debra D'Arcy 2004

ISBN 0 263 83820 X

Set in Times Roman 10½ on 12½ pt.
02-0404-39769

Printed and bound in Spain
by Litografia Rosés, S.A., Barcelona

CHAPTER ONE

RICK couldn't place her.

She stood in the foyer by the front desk, almost as stiff as the black business suit she wore. A red folder was pressed close to her white shirt, her attention on scanning the busy room.

She looked all business, except for her hair… Rick tilted his head and furrowed his brow. It was short, dark and tousled, sticking out at wild angles, looking like a style that belonged on an artist or a model, not on such a serious looking woman.

He rubbed his jaw. Odd.

He knew all of his own staff intimately, the research subsidiary by name and the support team on sight. Was she a new employee or just a passer-by?

Rick shook himself. She wasn't going to be a mystery. Two minutes and he'd have the young woman sorted, classified and pigeon-holed, like everything else in his life. He turned, focusing on the task at hand.

Rick straightened his tie and stepped up on to a chair, putting a smile on his face. 'I'd like to congratulate everyone here on a job well done—the Hinney & Smith project has been a great success for us. We can now ship our products all over the continent ourselves, cutting costs and increasing our profit margins.'

'We're now a bigger and better company and I'm proud of all of you.' He lifted his champagne glass. 'To a great team with a bright and prosperous future.'

He took a gulp of the champagne amidst the cheers and whistles. He meant it too. They were a great bunch to work with. Their dedication and loyalty to research, finance and ultimately acquisition had ensured his company another success.

His gaze wandered back to the cool but pretty stranger. The woman stood in the doorway, casually surveying his employees.

She didn't have a glass. He could remedy that.

Rick stepped down, smiling and shaking the hands of his team. He loved giving praise where praise was due—and hell, they all deserved heaps.

Rick rubbed his jaw. His next challenge was to merge the company with SportyCo, making his sports equipment twice the force in the marketplace. It was a risk to go for it so soon, but he couldn't wait. He wanted it. He hadn't worked so hard for the last ten years to baulk now.

It would probably be safer to wait, ensuring his playboy image was well behind him before he embarked on the ambitious move. It was unlikely that they'd agree to him as president of the combined company if he didn't have the right sort of credibility.

The last six months with Kasey Steel *should* have done the trick in convincing the world that he'd left his wild days behind him. His friends were believing that he'd settled down. The business world couldn't be far behind…?

No matter what he'd done he hadn't been able to free himself from his past. His passion for extreme sports was seen as reckless, his nights out with the boys as drunken rages and his dating as womanising. He couldn't win. Until now.

Rick hadn't expected the effect a steady relationship could have on his reputation. Though nothing could have got in the way of him doing the right thing by his friend. But now, here was a bonus, his chance to finally shake his infamous exploits of years ago and be taken seriously.

He had it made. He just had to stay on track. Rick's gaze darted back to the doorway. Right after he sorted out this woman.

He straightened his burgundy shirt and tightened his purple tie, smoothing down the silk. He buttoned his suit jacket, looking down at his matching black trousers. He'd pass.

He plucked another champagne glass from the table and weaved his way to the front desk, his eyes not leaving the newcomer.

She was taller than he'd first thought, almost as tall as himself in her black high heels. Her hair wasn't as wild or riotous on closer inspection. The 'do' looked as engineered as the rest of her. It was orderly and precise—only a pretext of rebellion.

What was she? An accountant from the finance department? A wayward librarian? Or some starched schoolteacher with aspirations of becoming a cold fish? She certainly was working the image.

He hesitated. He was half tempted to turn on his heel and melt into the crowd, allowing himself the luxury of speculation about the woman a little longer, entertaining himself with the possibilities.

She turned towards him, her dark eyes stabbing him. She was striking!

Rick strode forward and thrust the glass of champagne towards the stranger. 'You look lost,' he blurted like an idiot.

She smiled at him, putting up her hand and shaking her head at the glass. 'No thanks. And no, not at all.' She looked past him. 'I'm exactly where I should be.'

Rick took a quick sharp breath, unable to tear his eyes off the woman. He hadn't expected the vibrancy of her voice, the sweet lilt in her tone, or the brilliance in her dark eyes. There was no way she was as cool and controlled as she appeared to be.

His gaze slid over her, the chatter in the room fading, his breathing becoming louder, and his body becoming extremely aware of hers.

Rick cleared his throat, deftly discarded the drinks on a desk and moved into her line of sight.

She raised her dark eyes slightly to meet his, with an intensity that was discomfiting, as though she knew things that he wasn't privy to. 'I'm here for an appointment,' she said smoothly, glancing at the empty receptionist's desk. 'But I think that's the last thing on everyone's mind.'

'I could help,' he offered.

'Ye—es…' She pursed her lips and tried to look past him. 'Only if you can tell me where I can find Mr Keene.'

Warmth filled his body. He couldn't help but smile. 'You've found him.'

She looked taken aback for a moment as though he'd surprised her. She ran her dark gaze over him in a lazy perusal, from his black shoes, up his tailored suit, over his shirt and tie to his face.

Her eyes narrowed, searching his face as though try-ing to find the answer to a puzzle of her own.

Rick caught and held her gaze. 'Do I measure up?'

'Oh…sorry…of course.' Her cheeks flushed.

He stood taller. 'You were expecting someone else?'

'I didn't expect you to be so old.'

'Old?' What the—? 'I don't think thirty-four is old.' Had his face dried and cracked up since this morning's shave? Had a decade or three been stolen from his life? Admittedly, he no longer had the round, smooth features he'd had as a teenager. He rubbed his jaw. But he looked after himself.

She shrugged. 'I'm sorry. I didn't mean…' She pressed her lips together and looked away. 'I'm sorry to interrupt your celebrations. I could come back later?'

He put up a hand to stall her. 'No. It's not a problem.' But what about him being old? A person couldn't just blurt out a thing like that and not explain, especially not a young, pretty woman like this one, even if she was hiding being a cool façade.

'So…?' she asked softly. 'Which way would be your office? I presume you'd like to talk somewhere a little quieter?'

'Sure.' His muscles tightened. What could this be about? Dammit. He scanned the room for his secretary, his mind toying with the possibilities. Usually she would have informed him of his appointments for the afternoon before he'd gone out for lunch. Today, he'd sprung the celebration on the office…

He walked down the hallway, vividly aware of the woman behind him, of her softly scented perfume and of the mystery that shrouded her.

Where was she from? Who did she work for? What was her job? He could usually pick at least a person's occupation.

Rick opened the door to his private office and watched her pass him without a hesitation, her hips swaying gently. She moved as though she was in absolute control, with a musical rhythm, as though she was a dancer.

He rubbed his chin. *Who was she?* He strode into his large corner office. 'Patrick Keene,' he offered, holding out his hand. 'And you are?'

'Tara Andrews.' She shook his hand firmly, meeting his eyes with a calm assurance.

The name meant nothing. Neither, he assured himself, did the jolt deep in his gut at her firm touch.

Rick turned on his heel and strode around his large teak desk and glanced out at the Sydney skyline. He turned to face the woman. 'So?'

She barely glanced around at her surroundings. 'I'm here about your proposal.'

He sighed, dropping his shoulders. Mystery over. She was just work. 'Which one?' He moved to the desk and flicked through the papers scattered across the surface.

'Which one?' she echoed.

'Which proposal are you here to discuss, Miss?'

'I—'

'I have several projects in the pipeline—do you represent an investor or one of the parties involved?' He steeled himself for the concerns, the judgements, the resentments and/or the litigious threats that would come next.

'I'm not here for business,' she said in a more gentle tone. 'I'm here on a personal basis.'

He stared at her, his mind racing. Personal? *How* personal? There was no way he'd forget those deep dark eyes, those full red lips, her smooth tanned skin or her slender body, with curves that itched to be explored.

His body heated.

'I'm a proposal planner. Mr Thomas Steel asked me to come and tell you about my service in the hope that I could assist you in giving his daughter a memorable proposal of marriage.' She leant forward and handed him her business card.

'Marriage?' he echoed, his mind numbing. He took the card and stared at the words on it, trying to clear his head.

Had old man Steel got sick of waiting? He was always on about how old he was getting and how he wanted to see grandchildren before he died. Rick tensed. Had he and Kasey reached the end of their ruse? He hoped not.

'Am I in the wrong place?' Tara glanced at a page in the folder. 'No. This is right. You are Patrick Keene, aren't you?'

He stared at her. 'Yes, but…' A *proposal* planner? He crossed his arms over his chest, clenching his jaw against the rush of blood to his ears.

How could anyone think that a successful and extremely competent businessman like himself couldn't handle a task as simple and straight-forward as a proposal of marriage?

Was old man Steel pulling his leg? Or didn't he think that he was up to the task on his own? Or was he just tired of waiting for his daughter to come up with a family and figured he needed a shove in the back.

Unbelievable!

She pulled a chair away from his desk, positioning it to face him where he stood and sat down, crossing her long legs and propping the folder on her lap, her skirt riding up her smooth thighs in a most discomfiting way.

She offered him a small smile. 'By the look on your face I'd have to say Mr Steel hasn't broached the subject with you yet.' She glanced at him with questioning eyes. 'I'm sorry. Mr Steel came to me and requested that I come and have a chat with you, to let you know that help is available…' Her voice faded. 'If you need it.'

He lifted his eyebrows, shooting the woman a sardonic look. There was no way in hell he'd need help to propose!

The woman bit her bottom lip. 'I understand you've been going out with his daughter for some time now?'

'Yes,' he said tightly.

'Of course, the most important thing is that you propose to your girlfriend in your own time, when you're ready…'

Rick let out the breath he'd been holding. 'Thank you. I appreciate your consideration. I think Thomas Steel may have forgotten that particular point.' And several others, especially that people prefer to live their own lives, not ones engineered by him.

'I did try to tell him.' She shrugged. 'But he insisted.'

'I know what that's like.'

She licked her lips, staring at her folder. 'I agreed to come and let you know that proposal planning is a new service that offers busy men like yourself the opportunity to employ a person—' she touched her chest '—like me, to help you with many aspects of your proposal.' She tapped her pen against the page in front of her.

'I don't need help proposing.'

She didn't hesitate. 'I understand that perfectly, but will you hear me out? Most men *do* rush into the proposal, following whatever misconception they have, mostly from television, mind you. They sell themselves short and their partners. After all, the proposal is as special, if not more so, than the wedding itself—a declaration of love and commitment that sets up your life together.'

Rick leant against the corner of his desk, his arms crossed, studying the proposal planner. She was nice to watch, and to listen to—and surely there was no harm in hearing her out.

She tapped the pen against her full red lips. 'I can help you in many ways. We have an extensive library of books that you could borrow—poetry books, books of love letters and romance phrase books, if you're having trouble with how you're going to present the big question.'

Rick couldn't tear his gaze away from those lips.

'And then, of course, I can assist with all the legwork of investigating prices and possible venues for your proposal—'

He pressed his lips together to stop the smile teasing the corners of his mouth. Was she for real?

'And then, of course, there are all the ideas on how exactly you'd like to propose—whether you want to jump out of an aeroplane and propose ten thousand feet above the world, with the wind rushing around you. Or on a tropical island in the moonlight with a thousand stars twinkling in the sky above you.' She glanced up at him, her eyes bright. 'Or at a romantic restaurant with the sweet aroma of exotic food and gentle music, and with her face lit by soft candlelight. Or on a yacht out on the ocean, as though you were the only two people in the world…'

He held up his hand, staring down at the planner. She was amazing! Daunting even. How could she be so cool, then suddenly light up with such passion? How could she hide it so efficiently?

That crop of hair that was standing in all directions made her all the more striking—it was hard to take his eyes off her. Off her hair, off her deep, dark eyes, off those lips and those long, long legs.

'I think that—' he said, swallowing hard, pushing down the rising heat in his body. 'That although it sounds like a great idea, it's not for me.'

She laid her hands in her lap, took a deep breath and looked up at him with cool dark eyes. 'Of course, Mr Keene.'

He cleared his throat, trying to shake off the urge to keep her around a bit longer. 'Thank you for coming in but I'm quite capable of handling a proposal on my own.'

She nodded. 'I suspected that from the first moment I saw you.'

'Sorry for all your trouble.' He put his hand in his inner jacket pocket, grasping his wallet. 'I'll compensate you for your time, of course.'

She put up a hand. 'No need.' She slid her pen into the spine of her folder. 'I understand perfectly. My service isn't for everybody.'

He strode to the door and grasped the cold metal handle tightly. Much as he admired her passion, he couldn't afford to entertain any thoughts about the woman and her service. Not now.

He held the door open. The last thing they needed

was someone asking questions about his personal life, and Kasey's.

'Thank you for your time, and good luck,' she said, standing up and smoothing the creases from her skirt, over her well-rounded hips and down her thighs.

Rick pressed his lips together, clamping down on the burning heat scorching through his veins. He wanted his to be the hands on her curves. Wanted her hands running over *him.*

She didn't move, her eyes deep and dark and dangerously intent on him, almost as though she knew what he was thinking.

He pulled at his tie.

'I wish you both every happiness,' she said smoothly, her sweet voice even.

'Thanks.' Rick wanted to kick himself for his faltering, for the lack of his usual cool detachment, for his body's traitorous response to her, and for the enticing mystery she offered.

Hell, for the first time in six months he was regretting forfeiting bachelor life for Kasey's scheme. 'Thank you for taking the time to see me, but I have to get back to the others,' he said smoothly.

'Bye.'

Rick lurched out of the doorway and strode down the hall. He had to get away from the disturbing woman before he did something he'd regret.

He hadn't expected this. Not at all. How on earth had Thomas Steel even found the woman? He didn't even know that proposal planners existed…What next?

He weaved his way into the throng of his employees, concentrating on the task at hand, trying to push the woman from his mind.

The planner had been a surprise. A tall, lovely one that had tested him. Cripes, and what a test! Rick dragged in a long deep breath. But she was finished and over.

She was *not* part of the plan.

CHAPTER TWO

'YOU are like the stars in the starry heavens. Like the water is to the wet flowers. Like a dream I want to have for ever.' He swallowed and shifted his weight on his knees. 'I would be honoured...I would be thrilled...I want you to be my wife.'

She shook her head slowly.

'You're like a rose... a bird I want to hold, like a Porsche with shining bodywork—'

'I don't think so...' she said gently.

'But—'

Tara bit her lip, looking down at her client, her chest tight. 'Maybe you should go home and think about it some more?'

He shook his head. 'No. I have to practise. I know you don't usually help with the words themselves, but I'm so hopeless when it comes to this sort of stuff.'

'You're doing—'

'No, I'm not.' Mr Faulkner looked up at her, his face creased in pain. 'I really need you to hear it and help me get it right.'

Tara nodded.

He sucked in a deep breath. 'I want you. I want to keep you. I want to wake up to your smiling face in the morning, and hold you tight every night. Be my wife. Please.'

'It could work...' Tara stood up and approached the poor guy, still kneeling, still staring at the chair where his sweetheart would be for the real thing.

He shook his head. 'I don't want it to *just* work, I want my proposal to rock her world.'

Tara stared at him. He was barely as old as she was. How did he think at twenty-six that he knew what he wanted? How did he know that he'd found his soul mate? That sharing a life with someone else was going to make his better?

'Get up and stretch for a bit,' she offered, looking down at her notes, unable to meet his eyes. 'You're doing...well.' And at least he was into it, unlike Mr Keene.

Patrick Keene. What a hunk, if you liked that clean-shaven, strong jawed, short back and sides, office dweller look. Tara tapped her pen against her lips. He did it well, even if the colour scheme of his clothes was a little out there.

She should have expected him to say no. The man was obviously sitting on top of the world with his gigantic office in one of Sydney's largest buildings, in that tailor-made suit that hugged his wide shoulders and accentuated his height and power.

He hadn't seemed like the type of man to seek assistance for anything, let alone a proposal.

She bit the end of her pen and stared out of the window to the parked cars on the side street. She often fantasised about what a rich and influential client could do for their business. In the few hours from when Mr Steel had come to see her, until the moment she had laid eyes on Patrick Keene, she'd thought it was finally coming true.

The family business of Camelot would have thrived from the compliments Steel would have given their services, become a bustling hub of activity, everything that she planned it to be, just far sooner.

Pulling together her family's talents, Tara had promised both her sisters and her mother all the security and success they were looking for. And with her at the helm she was sure their fledgling business would be a winner.

They'd just have to manage without Patrick Keene.

Did Patrick know that Miss Steel was the one? She turned around and looked at the young man mouthing words silently to the chair, practising. *This* guy couldn't seem to find the words that expressed what it was about his partner that touched him deeply enough for him to consider spending the rest of his life monogamously with her.

Did Mr Faulkner really believe she'd be *smiling* every morning? That she'd want him to hold her *every* night? After the third baby arrived, after he'd been out with the boys, after he'd forgotten to put out the trash again, or after he'd come home late from work for the umpteenth time without an explanation….

Tara strode back to her desk, breathing short and fast. She straightened the papers, lined up the telephone to the edge and rearranged the pens in the cup.

'We've been at this for an hour. I guess I've tortured you enough, Miss Andrews?'

Tara swung to face the man.

He stood up and straightened his trousers, his brow furrowed. 'I'm not going to give up, you know.'

She nodded. 'I think it would be good for you to work on it at home for a few days.' She walked to the bookshelf and pulled out a poetry book. 'You might find it helpful to read this and make notes about which words represent what you feel about your girlfriend.'

'Poetry?' He dug his hands deep into his pockets, nodding slowly, then slipped into his suit jacket and took the book. 'It couldn't hurt.'

Tara glanced at her watch and headed for the door. 'At least we have all the rest of the arrangements sorted out for you. You can give me a call and I'll organise things for you, or you can do it yourself. You've got all the information.'

'I have to get the words right first,' he said tightly.

'And you will.' She opened the door wide, offering him a smile of encouragement. 'I'll see you next Thursday.'

Tara closed the door after him, sagging against the timber. What had she got herself into?

When she'd first introduced the proposal planning she'd expected to be planning the venue, the flowers, the music and lighting—something not much different to helping her mother and her sister, Skye, with the wedding planning. But listening to the words themselves…no. It was the last thing she'd considered doing.

She should have expected it. On the wedding side, the choice of vows was often reviewed, the best man's speech screened, and sometimes even written for him, and the toasts at the reception were often tweaked when requested by the clients.

Tara walked back to her desk and dropped into the large red chair. Listening to the amazing sweet nothings they uttered, even his—she looked at the door—was getting to her, reminding her of what she didn't have.

She could get a boyfriend... But—

She looked around her office, all red and white, all hearts and romance. The perfect setting for helping everyone else's boyfriends who were too busy, or too romantically-challenged, to come up with the perfect proposal plans on their own.

She wished she could help herself.

She ran a hand over her face. It helped to be busy—have the business to run, the books to look after, the bills to pay, weddings to help organise with her sister or her mum. And now her proposal planning, something her sisters weren't already doing, could take up the rest of her time efficiently and effectively.

She loved that she could complement the business with another service, one all of her own. Men were good to deal with. Not too emotional, not too mushy or sensitive. Not like some of the women her sister, Skye, had to deal with in the wedding planning. And the mothers!

Tara flicked the page over on the folder on her desk and scanned the appointments for the wedding boutique, cataloguing her involvement.

She tapped her pen on her bottom lip. So many variables… How many more weddings could her mother and Skye take on without putting on more staff? When would Skye be at work full time? How could they cut costs but increase clientele? How were they going to pay for that advertising campaign they'd had done?

Tara bit the end of the pen. Maybe she shouldn't have pushed for them to move from their home base to these professional offices until they had more cash flow…

The rap on the door was sharp and short.

'Come in.'

Camelot's secretary-cum-receptionist walked in, a cup of steaming hot coffee in her hand. She was a young woman fresh out of college, running over with enthusiasm.

'Is Mr Faulkner getting better yet?' Maggie grinned. 'The way he's going his mystery woman will be eighty before he gets to proposing.'

Tara shrugged, trying not to smile at the girl's appraisal of the situation. He just didn't seem to have enough confidence in himself to follow through and his embarrassment seemed so acute that he'd kept all the details from Tara. Maybe just in case he mucked it up or lost the nerve altogether to go through with the proposal. 'It's the clients' choice on how private they choose to be about their lives.'

Maggie nodded, stepping to the desk. 'And how'd that new client go? The one where the father wanted you to give the bloke a hand?'

Tara took the cup from her, shaking her head. 'It was a no go.'

'Better luck next time, yeah?' Maggie chirped, spun on her heel and strode to the door. 'At least you have Mr Faulkner.'

When Mr Steel had turned up at her office Tara had been more than surprised. The patriarch of social circles in Sydney on her doorstep? It had been a shock. It was unreal, and very unusual for the father to be coming in, rather than the man himself.

She leant back in her chair. Tara had hung on the man's every word, trying to work out how the whole situation was possible. How could he know that Mr Keene was ready to propose? Or had Mr Steel just become sick of waiting for the man to get serious?

Mr Thomas Steel didn't seem like the sort of man that needed a lot of patience...

Tara picked up the cup of coffee and took a sip. How did Mr Steel think that a man like Mr Keene would ever accept help? Was it just blind hope in thinking that he could encourage the guy into a commitment to his daughter?

She felt for the man despite the wild-goose chase he'd sent her on. The way he spoke about losing his wife and being bewildered in the area of his daughter's personal life had touched her heart. Despite not having any idea, he was determined to ensure her happiness in any way he could.

Tara's chest constricted. She wished her own father

could have cared like this man obviously did about his daughter.

Tara closed the folder and slid it into the drawer. It was probably a good thing that Mr Keene hadn't agreed to her help. She wasn't afraid of a handsome man who had it all, but she wasn't happy with that strange feeling in the pit of her stomach when he had looked at her with his emerald green eyes.

It scared her right down to her toes.

CHAPTER THREE

TARA picked the phone up with one hand, still typing in the last figure of the week's expenses into the computer. 'Tara Andrews.'

'Tara, Steel here, returning your call,' he said easily. 'How did you go?'

The man himself. She sucked in her breath. 'I'm sorry, Mr Steel, but Mr Keene is quite happy to handle his own plans.'

'He is?'

'He was quite adamant.' Tara wiped the specks of dirt off the keyboard. She wished she could have given the doting father better news.

'You did tell him what you could offer? That you could take care of all the details so there'd be minimum disruption to him. That virtually all he'd have to do was get down on his knee and ask the question.'

'Not in not so many words.'

'What's a bit of his time to make sure that the special moment is going to be absolutely magical for my daughter?' the man huffed.

'I'm sorry, Mr Steel, but Mr Keene has made his decision. There's nothing I can do.'

'Okay. Understood.' He cleared his throat. 'I've been

thinking that it could be advantageous for you to meet the couple.'

'I don't think that's a good idea, sir,' she said evenly, the thought unsettling her. The last thing she wanted was to see the man and experience that feeling again, let alone with the woman who was his soon-to-be-bride.

'Of course she won't know who you are or what you're helping Patrick with, my dear.'

'But—' Wasn't the man listening? Didn't he hear that Patrick didn't want her help?

'You'll get an idea of the sort of person she is so that you can help Patrick with his proposal.'

She gripped the phone tightly. 'Mr Steel, he has said no to my help. My hands are tied.'

'Would you come anyway? It would mean a lot to me if you just gave him a little more time to think about it. He probably made a snap decision.'

Tara swallowed hard. Mr Keene may have done that all right. He'd made up his mind the moment she'd introduced herself—the look in his eyes had said it all.

She tapped her pen against her desk. Could it hurt to pander to Mr Steel? She didn't want the man to be upset on her account. 'I'm not making any promises,' she said slowly. '*If* Mr Keene comes to me and asks me for my help…'

'Great. Wonderful. There's a charity dinner tonight that we're all attending, which would be the ideal situation for you to meet him…them…us.'

'Tonight?' A knot formed deep in her stomach. 'This is rather short notice, sir.'

'If you can be there around seven. I'll add your name to the list.' He rattled off the address of one of Sydney's top hotels and hung up.

Tara stared at the phone, then at her computer screen.

She re-positioned herself in the chair, her muscles tight, an unpleasant queasiness brewing deep in her body.

She *had* to look on the bright side. Mr Steel had got what he'd wanted, for now, even though she couldn't see that she could do anything for a man as strong and confident as Patrick Keene. No meant no.

Tara glanced at her watch, jerking to her feet. She didn't have time to mull over her acceptance of the invitation. She'd just have time to get ready.

She picked up her handbag and jacket and strode to the door. She was stressing over nothing. All she would have to achieve tonight was to present a good image to Mr Steel, showing him her dedication and her commitment. So maybe when Mr Keene *did* get around to proposing, they'd use Camelot for the wedding.

She only hoped that Mr Keene didn't take her presence tonight the wrong way…his bark seemed as though it could be intense, and his bite lethal.

Rick slipped his arm around Kasey's shoulder and pulled her a little closer to him. It should have been second nature by now to play the role of Kasey's boyfriend, but he still felt awkward.

He didn't know whether it was because Kasey was

his best friend's little sister. Or because of the lies they were perpetrating.

At least they weren't hurting anyone.

Rick glanced at Steel. And it was about time that Kasey scored a few points of her own.

He smiled, trying to look casual, trying to look like he was enjoying being here with Kasey and her father. The only good here tonight was the chance to support the children's hospital.

The charity event was a full-on affair complete with a thirty-piece orchestra, ice sculptures and caviare. All the stops had been pulled out to woo the rich into delving deep into their pockets for the kids.

He'd never needed any encouragement.

Kasey elbowed him in the ribs. 'Lighten up, Rick.'

'I'm trying.' Rick looked down into Kasey's face, pretty and painted, soft and round, her hair all pulled up and elegant-looking.

'Try harder.'

Rick hadn't told Kasey about the proposal planner idea her father had come up with. It was hardly worth mentioning since he'd taken care of it. She probably would have chucked a fit at her father's interference, again.

What had possessed the man to come up with the crack-pot scheme? Help with proposing... He could do it with his eyes shut, if he cared to.

Sure, he hadn't thought of what he'd say to a woman, but it wasn't like he'd come close to wanting to. His relationships had always been fleeting.

'How's things with you?' Rick had hardly seen Kasey at all the past few weeks, their public outings being pruned back to the point of being non-existent.

'Good. Really good. You know that certain special someone...' She smiled warmly. 'I think I'm in love. Truly in love. He's amazing, sweet and totally wonderful.'

Rick smiled down at her bright face. 'So, you don't need me any more?'

She punched him gently on the shoulder, a grin on her face a mile wide. 'Come on. I'm not going to come clean just yet. I don't want Father to scare Jack away.'

Rick lifted an eyebrow. 'Your father hasn't scared me away.'

'Yet.' She shook her head. 'As far as my father's concerned you're not good enough for me either.'

'Probably not.' He had the sneaking suspicion that no one, ever, was going to be good enough for his daughter. It was one of the reasons he had decided to go through with this. Kasey would never find someone if the old man ran them all off before she'd had a chance to get to know them.

He pulled his shoulders back. Nothing could replace her brother in her life but he could be there when she needed him. It was the least he could do for his buddy's little sister.

He gritted his teeth. If only he could take back that night in their final year. If only he'd slowed Colin up on the drinking that night. If only he hadn't left the car keys where Colin could find them. He clenched his jaw.

When the police had come the next morning Rick had had no idea what was going on. He'd thought Colin was in bed, not wrapped around some tree down the road.

Asking him to make that promise to look after Kasey was the last thing his best friend had said to him. And there was no way on the planet that he was going to break it.

Kasey had only been twelve. Poor kid. And old man Steel, after losing his wife, then his only son, had gone all out to protect Kasey from everything, including life.

Kasey nudged him in the ribs, a grin on her face. 'You look like you're at a funeral. I know these things are dead boring—'

'But for a good cause.'

She rolled her eyes. 'Think of something happy.'

That proposal planner came to mind. The way she moved, the way she talked, the passion in her every word, her smile…

At any other time he'd have enjoyed peeling her cool, calculated layers until he found the vibrant woman that pulsed underneath. What a challenge it would be to re-lease the passion he saw in her eyes and heard in her voice, breaking away her cool crust entirely.

His body heated at the thought.

Kasey grinned. 'Much better.' She turned to face the room, drawing him closer to her as though they were posing for photos.

Rick cast a glance at her father, who was by the ice sculpture. He was leaning his stocky frame against the table, his snowy-white hair making him look more like Father Christmas than Attila the Hun.

Kasey looked up at him with wide eyes, chewing her thumb nail. 'I'm starting to think he knows something's up.'

'How?' They'd gone to great lengths to be seen around together, at all the right places, at just the right times to get noticed. And all the right gossip was being circulated. For Kasey, and for him.

'I have no idea. Maybe he feels there's no passion.' She pouted. 'You know how Dad loves to interfere in my life, so please make this good. Or my life is going to be hell again.'

'Sure. Of course I can.' It wasn't much to ask really. He could do this. Acting like her serious boyfriend was nothing to give her some peace. And if it secured him a reputation and the presidency of the merged companies, all the better.

He cupped Kasey's face and looked down softly into her eyes, thinking of wild hair cuts, deep dark eyes and deep red lips.

'I should probably say something really romantic to make you blush,' he said softly to her.

'Yep.'

Rick leant closer. 'What do you give an elephant with big feet?' he whispered. 'A lot of room.'

Kasey giggled and fell into his arms. 'Dope—'

Rick held her, smiling. He scanned the lavish room, the marble pillars of the foyer obscuring his view of the milling people.

The men were all suited, as he was, in black. The women were richly dressed in fine gowns and fur wraps with heavy jewellery glittering left, right and centre.

Steel kept glancing in his direction. He was either sizing him up for a coffin or as a prize on his mantelpiece. Rick shifted awkwardly; neither felt good.

Rick looked over Kasey's head to the foyer, slipping his hand into his pocket and gripping his car keys tightly. Would anyone notice if they left—? If this relationship were for real they would have slipped out of this stiff affair and found somewhere quieter, with soft lights and romantic music.

His breath caught in his throat. Could he be dreaming?

The proposal planner stood in the foyer, her body moulded by a white dress that clung to her curves like a second skin. The fabric stopped just below her knees, her feet were in white heels, a light wrap was draped around her shoulders, a plain gold chain around her neck.

Her hair was as wild as ever, and a deep red lipstick made her lips all the more alluring.

She looked amazing. She stood tall, her chin up and her eyes drifting across the people in the room. Cool and aloof and in total control.

Tara Andrews.

Heat flooded his body. She was disturbing in every way. Hell. He took several deep breaths, trying to quell his body's response and act like the devoted boyfriend and not as though his interests were straying.

The chatter in the room subsided. Rick tore his eyes from her to glance around him. There was more than one man intrigued by this surprise arrival.

No matter how cool her façade, there was no camouflaging her powerful presence, her height or her curves in that dress.

What the hell was she doing here?

Thomas Steel walked to her side without hesitation, leaning close, his white hair almost touching her cheek. The look of pure delight on the old man's face stabbed Rick deep in the chest. What was he up to?

She smiled.

Rick's gut pulled tight.

Thomas touched her elbow and steered her through his guests, directly towards them.

Rick sucked in his breath. What was going on? He stiffened. He stared at the painting on the far wall instead, avoiding looking at the newcomer. The naked busty woman did little to distract him—the art was rich and overdone.

The colours of the painting blurred. He'd just have to do his best to ignore the planner's allure and what she did to his body.

Steel clapped him on his shoulder. 'I'd like you to meet Tara, a friend of mine. This is my daughter, Kasey, and her boyfriend, Patrick.'

Rick forced himself to move, to smile, to breathe. His attention drifted to her face.

Tara's eyes were shining with a steadfast calm and serene assurance. 'Hello.'

'Nice to meet you, Tara,' Kasey said, running her gaze over the woman, then glancing at Rick.

'Likewise,' Tara offered, her voice warm, moving her attention from Kasey to him casually.

Rick swallowed. 'Pleased to meet you, Tara.'

Tara lifted an eyebrow, feeling the rise of heat in her cheeks, her name on his lips coursing through her veins like molten lava.

She took his hand, grasping it, forcing a smile. He felt good... and strong...and warm...and his touch made her skin tingle.

Patrick gripped her hand more tightly. 'Have you and Thomas known each other long?'

'Oh...ages,' Mr Steel injected. 'I'll leave you two to look after our newest guest.' And he winked at her.

She extricated her hand from Patrick's, stroking her palm against her hip as though she was smoothing her dress, trying to dispel the buzz of sensation on her skin.

This was crazy. She shouldn't have come. She liked being in her office and offering advice, not being dragged into the field.

And what a field. This place was incredible. With tall columns through the enormous rooms.

The ceilings inside had to be at least three metres high, the cornice elaborate, the walls painted a rich lemon colour and adorned with golden-framed paintings and mirrors.

Tara stepped a little further away from the couple, closer to the marble statue of a naked woman carrying a jug. She feigned an interest in the unusual sofas, with sculpted edges that resembled wings and a deep blue upholstery dotted with gold and edged with a matching brocade.

Everything was decorated lavishly, including Miss Steel.

Tara forced herself to face the woman who had captured Patrick Keene's heart. She could have been a model—her chestnut hair was swept up to the top of her head, diamond encrusted earrings dangled from her ears and she wore a black dress that was to die for. And the emerald green silk wrap was exquisite. As she was.

She had everything. A father devoted to her, and a man like Patrick Keene in love with her, about to ask her to share his life with him.

Tara swallowed hard, trying to still the needs stirring deep inside her. She couldn't begrudge Kasey having the perfect life, and she couldn't let this singe her hard-won control.

'How do you know my father?'

She looked across the room to where Thomas Steel was merrily chatting to a group of people. She hadn't expected this. She'd thought she'd be observing the loving couple from afar, not thrown amongst them like fresh meat to the wolves.

'How do I know your father?' Tara repeated, her mind scrambling for an answer. 'Business.'

'What sort of business?' Kasey asked.

Tara shot Patrick a look. 'You could say I'm a problem solver.'

Patrick crossed his arms in front of his chest. 'And if people don't want their problems solved?'

His words impaled her. He must think she was stalking him! 'Then they're not going to call me,' she said as calmly as she could.

'And if someone else does?' Patrick asked, his voice deep and velvet smooth.

'Then the person that called me must care a lot,' Tara said easily. 'But I can't help if the client doesn't want any help.'

'Well, this is all fascinating and terribly obvious.' Kasey fanned herself with her hand. 'But I think I need a drink. Are you coming, Rick?'

'In one minute,' Rick offered, smiling at his girlfriend and then turning to Tara, as though he was dealing with nothing more significant than tying a loose shoe-lace, or swatting a fly or squashing a bug.

Kasey shrugged and sauntered towards the bar.

A tense silence enveloped them.

She stared at Patrick's mouth, pressed thin, her breath solidifying in her throat. She didn't want to be the bug! No matter how tall, dark or rich he was.

CHAPTER FOUR

PATRICK closed the space between them. 'What are you doing here?' he whispered harshly.

Tara dragged in a deep breath, her mind scrambling, his spicy scent invading her senses, the power he was exuding dangerously intense. 'I *was* invited.'

'Why?'

Tara sighed. 'Mr Steel insisted that I give you one more chance. I think he was hoping that maybe you'd thought about what I said earlier and have changed my mind.'

Rick shook his head. 'You could have warned me you'd be popping up all over the place.'

'I'm sorry, I didn't—' She looked at the ceiling. 'I didn't get a lot of notice myself. I'm sorry.'

'Another one of the old man's great ideas?'

'Yes…I'm sorry to intrude, Mr Keene. There was no intention to put you on the spot with Miss Steel.' She tried to keep her voice as impartial as she wanted to feel. 'I didn't expect—'

'Call me Rick.'

She stiffened. 'Pardon?'

'I said call me Rick. I can't stand all this Mr Keene stuff. You make me feel like my father.'

'Fine, Rick,' she said, trying it out. It felt great. It

suited him. 'Rick' suited his wild ties and colourful shirts like the one he wore now. A silver tie against a royal purple shirt with a black dinner suit. 'I wouldn't want to make you feel old.'

'That reminds me, you said I was old when we first met.' His voice was deep and low, his green eyes intent on her.

She couldn't help but smile. At least something she'd said had registered. 'Yes, I did. Sorry.'

He moved closer to her. 'Are you going to explain yourself or are you going to drive me mad wondering what in hell you meant?'

She shrugged, standing her ground. 'I meant just what I said. I hadn't expected you to be so old.'

He rubbed his jaw, straightening to his full height. 'You think I'm old?'

'No. I don't, in general.' She hesitated, looking up into his handsome face. He seemed perfect. 'It's just that I hadn't expected Miss Steel to be marrying someone like you, that's all.'

Rick crossed his arms over his chest, looking down into her face, his eyes narrowed. 'And why is that?'

'There must be at least ten years between you two and, from what I've read of her, she doesn't usually go for the mature, older type.'

Rick opened his mouth and closed it. 'Well, she did.'

Tara nodded, her insides twisting. 'Yes, she did.' She lifted her chin and met his gaze. 'There's no point in asking you why you go for her...'

'Really, because you know that I won't answer you?'

'No.' She couldn't help but smile. 'Because she's a beautiful young rich heiress.'

He frowned. 'And which part do you think *I'm* particularly interested in?'

She bit her lip. Damn. What had possessed her to just blurt out what was on her mind? Her mind fluttered. 'Kasey as a beautiful person?'

Rick's eyes glittered.

She swallowed hard. Would he accept her diplomatic save or push her on the matter? The last thing she wanted to do was admit she was jealous of the girl.

'What are you two talking about?' Kasey shoved a drink towards Rick. 'You two look so cosy—you'd better be careful or someone will think you two came together.' Kasey shot Rick an accusing glare.

Tara lifted her chin, her blood cooling. 'Not at all. Just passing the time with small talk.' Damn, she'd totally forgotten where she was and what she was meant to be doing!

She stepped backwards.

Kasey draped herself around Rick and laughed softly. 'Of course, Rick only has eyes for me. Don't you, honey?'

He looked down at her, sighing deeply. 'Absolutely.'

Tara turned away. Her solitary existence ripped through her, leaving a deep and hollow ache in her chest.

She watched the other guests in the room happily chatting, her hands clenched tightly in front of her. Should she escape now, or see this through?

What did Kasey think of her being so chummy with her boyfriend? She was meant to be a professional after all. She glanced at the heiress.

The woman seemed oblivious to the situation, cooing over Rick as though nothing had happened. Either she was too clever to challenge what she'd seen, or too blinded by love.

Tara prayed for the latter. The last thing she wanted was a rich and influential socialite assassinating Camelot's reputation because she couldn't keep her eyes off her boyfriend and her mind on work.

Thomas Steel tapped Tara on the shoulder. 'Would you do me the honour of allowing me to introduce you around?'

'Of course,' she blurted. Saved. She'd pretend Rick Keene didn't exist and concentrate on Thomas Steel. Then Kasey would have no concerns about her and Rick, and Camelot would live happily ever after.

Tara looped her arm through Mr Steel's. 'Nice meeting you both,' she offered the couple.

Mr Steel led her into the crowd, leaning close to her. 'What do you think?'

Tara looked at the man. 'About what?'

'About Patrick Keene…and my daughter.'

She swallowed, resisting the urge to look back at them and take one last look at Rick Keene. 'A lovely couple.'

'Right.' He stroked his chin as though he'd once had a beard. 'He's…he's a…fine man.'

'Yes. Seems to be.' If not a little too arrogant, handsome and self assured for her liking. 'He knows his mind.'

Mr Steel grimaced. 'I'm not so sure.'

Tara turned to the man, trying to keep a straight face, acutely aware of his scrutiny. How could he delude himself into thinking a man in charge of such a large and successful company didn't know his own mind?

'Mr Steel, if you think I'm going to chase after the man, trying to convince him to use my services, I'm going to have to disappoint you,' she said evenly. 'He doesn't want or need my assistance.'

Mr Steel's eyes glinted. 'That's a pity. You're so suited…' He glanced backwards.

Tara refused to take the bait. As far as she was concerned her business here was done. 'Take this.' She handed him one of her business cards. '*If* he does decide to go ahead with a proposal and is thinking of getting some assistance, tell him to give me a call.'

She glanced at her watch, her attention wandering annoyingly back to the couple, who were in close conversation. Rick was leaning close to Kasey, his arm around her waist. A soft smile was on her face. 'Good luck with your charity event,' Tara blurted.

'You're not staying?'

Tara shook her head. She'd had enough for one night. There was no point hanging around, torturing herself with dreams of clients that weren't to be, soul-mates who never appeared or fantasies that never could come to pass.

She looked at the doorway.

If Rick Keene wanted her help, he'd have to come to her…and the chances of that were a billion to one against. And, for the first time in her life, she was happy with the odds.

He was too perfect for her own good.

Rick watched old man Steel steer Tara into the throng of people, his head bent close to hers in quiet conversation. What was he cooking up now?

Rick glanced at Kasey, his neck stiff and his hands clenched by his sides. He'd protect her no matter what her father came up with next.

Kasey put her hands on her hips, turning to him, her eyes narrowed and her lips pouting. 'So who is she? You two nearly ruined everything with Father.'

'I didn't think.' Rick rubbed his jaw. 'But you don't have to worry about your father getting the wrong idea about Tara and me.'

'Why?' Kasey swung around and stared after her father and Tara, who were standing in a corner on the other side of the room, looking for all the world like conspirators.

His neck muscles tensed.

'Are you ready for this?' He crossed his arms over his chest. 'I know her.'

Kasey grinned. 'Don't tell me she's an ex-girlfriend who gave you the flick?'

He stiffened. 'Why do you say that?'

'Because you're all ape-faced over her.' Kasey's mouth quirked into a mischievous grin.

He shook his head. 'No way.'

She laughed. 'And it's so rare for a woman to dump you. I figure she's the one that got away.'

'No, she isn't.' Rick slipped his hands into his trouser pockets, shrugging off the ripple that coursed through him. 'She's a proposal planner.'

'What?'

'Your father hired her in the hope that I'd agree to use her services so I'd propose to you properly.'

'Propose? Wow…' She giggled. 'Daddy—you have to love him for his dedication to the role. But do you really think he's accepted I'm going to marry you?'

'Sounds like it.' Rick couldn't bring himself to be as touched by the sentiment as Kasey obviously was.

'What do you think we should do? Proposing sounds serious…' She bit the end of her thumbnail. 'But I'm not ready to break this all off. Are you?'

Rick shook his head. 'I could do with another week or two.'

'Me, too.'

Rick rubbed his jaw. 'Then I should play along with this proposal stuff.'

'It couldn't hurt.'

'No, it couldn't.' Rick mulled over his meetings with the SportyCo company about the merger, flashes of Tara Andrews's fine eyes and deep red lips invading his thoughts. 'And agreeing to this proposal plan business would…buy us some time.'

'Yes. I can't have him suspect what's really up.' Kasey

shook her head, sobering. 'There's no way I want him grilling Jack, pressuring him or sacking him.'

'Are you sure he'll be hard on Jack?'

'I know my father. The only reason that he's tolerating you is because you're as close as I've come to his idea of what a good prospect is for me. He'll probably be sizing you up as the father of my children too...'

'And although I'm cute...'

'Ugh, not a chance.' Kasey shook her head, grinning. 'But if he suspects there's no passion between us and his chance of grandkids is zilch...he could do anything.'

'So, I'll get on to that proposal planning service and do my best to up the passion quota with you in public so he gets the idea we're fine in that department.'

'God, no.' Kasey stepped back, her eyes wide, a smile tugging at the corners of her mouth. 'I'm not going to waste the time you buy us by spending time with you.'

'True.' He nodded, wrapping his arm around hers. 'Jeez, you make me feel so loved.'

'Ha ha.'

Rick couldn't help but smile with her. If he had a little sister Kasey would be just like her. And it was great to know he was helping. 'So I just do the proposal planning thing?' His mind darted to the idea of spending time with Tara Andrews. His pulse pounded, a heat spreading through his veins like wildfire.

'Absolutely. If you can manage it. But can you stand to spend time with that Tara woman?' she lilted.

Rick stiffened. Were his thoughts that transparent? 'I think I can bear it, for a little while.'

'I'm sure you will.' Kasey grinned. 'But remember, you've got a couple of weeks before you're a bachelor again so watch what you do and say.'

'Sure. Not a problem.' He rubbed his jaw. 'But I can't imagine this proposal stuff is going to take that long.'

Kasey looked up at him, her eyes wide. 'Why not?'

'Come on, it wouldn't be too hard for me to pick a place to propose and decide on the arrangements needed. Jeez, I've been to enough places with enough women to know—'

'Well, make it hard. String it out. We can't have the planner getting you all organised in a couple of days... I need at least a week or two.'

'Me, too.' Rick shifted his weight, drawing Kasey closer, his arm around her waist. He leant close to her, whispering in her ear as a group of people moved past them. 'But...how am I going to find the time to do the planning stuff when I'm going to be flat out with the merger for the next week?'

Kasey turned her head slightly towards him. 'I'm sure you'll manage to fit her into your busy schedule with minimal disruption to you.'

Minimal disruption! Rick watched Tara across the room, near the entrance, sliding a hand down the fabric of her gown and over her curves.

She was going to be a major disruption to his entire being! And he couldn't wait...

CHAPTER FIVE

'GOOD morning, honey.' Tara's mother pushed back a stray wisp of hair to the mother-of-pearl clip at her nape. 'The Donalds have decided on the Hilton. The Gregory clan want to change their dates for the wedding to June. And the cake for the Wilson wedding is one tier short—' her mother glanced at her watch '—and I'm on my way in five minutes to oversee their wedding.'

'Right, Mum.' Tara didn't break stride as she moved through the front office. 'I'll book the Hilton. I'll talk to the church and reception centre about changing the Gregory wedding and get back to you. And I'll ring the bakery and see what they can offer the Wilsons as compensation for their error.'

'Thanks.' Her mother gathered up her folder, her bag and coat. 'Oh, and I think that nice concierge at the All Seasons Hotel is going to ask you out.'

Tara froze in her tracks. Not again. 'What did you say?'

'Nothing much. Just that you're a beautiful young lady, and still single.'

'Mum!' What was she going to do with her? For some insane reason her mother was trying to arrange her love life, as if Tara didn't have enough to worry about.

'So, will you go out with him when he asks you?'

Tara crossed her arms and shot her mother a glare. 'No, Mum. One, he's a head shorter than me. Two, he's not my type and three, I'm too busy.'

Her mother took her hand, looking up into her face. 'What you do around here is wonderful, honey. We've come so far, but don't forget you need a life too. It's really nice for a girl to be loved.'

Tara lowered her eyes. 'I've got a heap to do.' They'd be a lot further with the business if it hadn't been for girls wanting love.

Her youngest sister, Riana, had nearly ruined them all before they'd started by romancing a handsome man in the wedding party—he'd been the groom, and the affair had broken up the first wedding they'd secured as a family.

Skye's search for love had affected them too. She still hadn't got back to focusing on her career after getting involved with the wrong man, and that was years ago now.

Tara shivered. And her own experiences with men had only served to distract her from the job at hand rather than help her life. No matter how much she liked the guy the relationships ended up demanding or disastrous.

Now was not the time.

'Think about it, darling,' her mother said, sauntering out of the door, her eyes suspiciously bright.

Tara couldn't think about it, wouldn't think about it. She didn't want anything to do with anyone. She needed to stay focused and one-tracked. Nothing she was going to do was going to jeopardise all their hard work or divert her attention from the business. It needed her.

'Morning, Maggie,' Tara chimed, lifting her chin and shrugging off the uneasy feeling in the pit of her stomach. 'Any mail? Calls?'

'Sure.' The girl swished her blonde hair off her shoulder. 'Calls from the Halls, Robertsons, Taylors, Millers and the Forsythes. And the mail for your attention.' She handed her a clump of envelopes, tied neatly in a red bow.

'Thanks.' Tara took the bundle and strode to her office. She dropped the letters on her desk, slipped into her seat and picked up the phone.

Being the assistant for both wedding planners was a full-time job as well as proposal planning but she wouldn't give up her new little branch of the business for anything…

She flicked the letters open in between calls, trying to concentrate on the work at hand and not on last night.

Rick Keene's tall, solid frame invaded her mind, the image of his brilliant green eyes making her body warm.

So, there was a way about him that pushed her buttons; it was nothing special, he was a charmer. So, there was an intelligent man beneath the tailored power suit, who liked arty ties, no big deal. So, she sort of liked his strength and arrogant power—he'd said no and she wouldn't have to ever think about him again.

She swallowed hard. And that was a good thing.

There were plenty of other rich bachelors in the city who could knock on her door and want her help...

A knock echoed through the room.

Tara jerked her head up. Was it as easy as thinking about rich bachelors? She wished!

The door swung open.

Rick stood in her doorway, his dark hair neatly combed, his face clean-shaven and his crisp shirt a deep purple that contrasted with a lemon-coloured tie with purple squares floating on it.

Tara opened her mouth but no words would come.

'May I come in?' he asked, his deep voice resonating through her. He stepped in and closed the door behind him, his gaze sweeping over her.

She had the insane urge to straighten her trouser suit, smooth out her white shirt and cover the thrust of her breasts with her jacket or her arms.

Her intercom beeped. 'Tara, a Mr Keene is here to see you.'

'Mr Keene?' Tara croaked. What she would have given for Maggie to have buzzed a little sooner, or for Rick to have dallied a little in the hall.

He reduced the distance between them and dropped into the chair opposite her desk as though he was as at home in her office as he would have been in his. 'Miss Andrews... Tara.'

Her stomach curled at his deep warm voice. What did *he* want? She pressed her lips together.

His eyes glittered. 'I believe you were going to call me by my first name.'

She straightened the papers in front of her and placed them into a pile to one side of her desk, breathing deep and slow. 'Ye—es,' she said slowly. 'But I also thought you'd said *no* to my services.'

'I did.' He looked around her office, his perusal slow and assessing.

Tara was painfully aware of how small her office was in comparison to his. Hers was chock-full of filing cabinets, with a desk and a couple of chairs squashed in for good measure, to make it look more like an office and less like the storeroom it served as. And her ruby red and white colour scheme was far from the conservative creams and greys in his.

She stared at his yellow tie and mauve shirt. Was there a frustrated artist in him that hadn't been let loose on his office yet?

She crossed her arms, watching him take in all the romantic knick-knacks she'd placed strategically around the office—champagne glasses on the shelf, little glass hearts hanging at the window, vases of red roses and a bowl of heart-shaped chocolates.

The photos on the walls were the finishing touch. Photos of weddings—on lawns, in churches, and by the sea…Camelot's couples—the ones her family had helped make their dreams come true.

'You did say no.' She eyed him carefully. 'And now?'

Rick leant forward, leaning his elbows on his knees, clasping his hands together. 'Now… I'm thinking I'd like to discuss this proposal planning with you. I may have been a little hasty yesterday.'

'You sounded adamant to me.' She tilted her head slightly, trying to feel what was really going on. This didn't make sense. He wasn't anything like her typical client…

'I was. Then I got to thinking that a little help here and there wouldn't hurt.'

'So you *are* thinking of proposing to Kasey?'

Rick cast a long look out of the window behind where she sat as though he didn't want to meet her eyes. 'Yes.'

Tara regarded him carefully, stiffening. 'And you'd like my help?'

'Yes.'

'You surprise me.'

The beginning of a smile tipped the corners of his mouth. 'I'm full of surprises.'

Tara darted him a look. She bit her lip and sorted through her pencil container, fighting the warmth spreading through her body.

This is what she had dreamed of—a rich bachelor wanting her help—but the reality was far more daunting… She'd have to spend time with the man, talk to him about the woman he loved, plan the romantic moment with him and set it up. The reality stank.

He leant forward, fighting a smile. 'I assure you I don't bite.'

She let out the breath she had been holding. 'And I assure you that I'm not scared of you.'

'Oh?'

'Not at all.' She stood up, looking down into his emerald eyes with as much cool and calm as she could muster. She glanced at her watch. 'When would you like to get started.'

She could do this. She just had to instruct him in a great proposal. Easy. She picked up the papers off her desk and held them close to her. With her checklists, her contacts, her experience and her tried and true strategy she'd have him on his knees in no time at all.

She crossed her fingers under the papers she was holding and shot a prayer ceiling-ward. 'I could fit you in now.' And get it over and done with as quickly and as efficiently as possible.

Rick stood up, smoothing down his trousers and straightening his tie. 'Sorry. No can do. I was just passing through and thought I'd call in and let you know I'd go ahead with it.'

'You could have phoned.'

He hesitated. 'I could have…but…as I said, I was passing through.'

'Okay. When would be convenient for you?'

'I have no idea.' He shrugged. 'I'll have to talk to my secretary.'

'Great. Okay. Just give me a call when you know and I'll try to squeeze you into my busy schedule.' There was no reason to think that she was going to bend over backwards for him just because he was rich, influential and dashing.

'Right.' He strode to the door, flung it wide and stepped out, closing the door firmly behind him.

Tara sagged into her seat, propping her elbows on the desk. Thank God *that* was over. She glared at the intercom. Next time she'd have Maggie keep him in Reception, give her time to prepare for him—if anyone could prepare for a force like that.

She bent over, resting her face in her hands. He was not going to catch her off-guard again!

The door swung open. 'Five on Monday is good for me, what about you?' Rick said casually as he stuck his head around the door.

'You just…called her?' Tara bit her lip. Cripes, this was a man of action-and-a-half.

He waved his mobile phone next to his head. 'Great invention.'

'Ye—es.' She stared at him, her mind struggling to understand what on earth was going on. One day he was totally off the idea, now he was totally on. 'Fine. Okay. Five is fine.'

'Yes, that works,' he said into the phone. 'Thanks for your help. I'll be in within the hour.' Rick snapped the phone shut and slipped it into his suit pocket. 'I know it's a lot to ask, but I'm a really busy man…'

Tara froze in her seat. Now what?

'Could we meet at my office? The traffic to get here was hell and I could really do with every minute at work.' He shot her a devastating smile, his eyebrows rising slightly and his eyes glittering deep and bright and brilliant.

She dragged in a quick breath. 'Sure.'

Rick gave her a curt nod and slipped out of the door, closing it firmly behind him.

Tara leant back into her seat, her mind racing as fast as her pulse, relieved he'd finally left.

She stared at the door, biting her bottom lip. Had she just been hoodwinked by his charm?

She slapped the desk with her palm. Darn. She should have pushed for doing the session here... She'd never had to chase a client around before.

Tara sighed. At least she'd done the impossible—she'd got their first big client. And he wasn't just big. He was tall, rich and handsome, and he was going to propose to an heiress from a prominent Sydney family.

She would have walked over hot coals for a client like him. And, by the way Rick Keene was acting, she may just have to!

CHAPTER SIX

TARA closed her apartment door, slipped her keys back in her bag and hung it on the hook by the door. She placed her folder on the hallstand, and leant heavily on the wall.

There was nothing like coming home.

The three red cushions on her bone-white sofa were centred, lined up perfectly and overlapping each other by exactly a third of their width.

Her Persian rug, which didn't have a speck of fluff on it, sat squarely on the floor; her sparkling glass-topped mahogany coffee table on top was completely parallel to the sofa.

The magazine she'd been reading last night still sat on the dining table, aligned with the edge of the white marble surface.

Each of the fruits in the red china dish was in place, every piece of furniture and every vibrant work of art on the walls exact and plumb.

Everything was as she'd left it this morning. She closed her eyes and breathed in the soft scent of the incense she burnt nightly. There was something in being single.

She slipped out of her shoes, lining them up under the hall table, and took off her jacket. Home. She liked having her own place, and her own space, and her own order, not someone else's.

And another tall, dark, handsome man was leaving bachelordom behind. She sighed deeply. One less left in the world.

Mr Keene's tailored suit, his deep purple shirt and his yellow tie had stated confidence and position today. His wide shoulders and deep chest suggested a fighting fit body underneath. And his shining green eyes and the way they'd perused her screamed trouble.

Her stomach clenched tight.

She shook herself. It was nothing. Keene was just a man. She was a woman. His looking at her so…intently… meant nothing. Nothing at all.

She was just being silly, her imagination working overtime in collaboration with her overactive hormones, putting all sorts of weird and unwelcome thoughts in her head, and her body.

It was all those romantic sweet nothings that she had to think about, and all the ideas that accompanied them. She just needed to hear a few of her own, whispered in her ear by a tall, dark and dashing male.

She managed to smile. As if that was a possibility when her life didn't seem to include time to relax any more let alone time for a boyfriend.

She straightened. No big loss. She'd had them before and they had never lived up to their promises. She was better off without them, and so was Camelot. The family business was enough for her now. It was the one thing she could rely on.

They could all rely on each other.

She hadn't planned to bring her family all together in one business after she'd finished college. She had a job as an office manager for an up-and-coming corporation, but when Skye had fallen in love, and in deep trouble, Tara had been driven to find a solution that would work for them all.

Her mother and Skye had been doing weddings for some time when Tara stepped in and banded the family together. They'd been scraping a living in weddings from home, by word of mouth and only just managing— now they were going to have a future.

She had built Camelot up into what it was today with a lot of sweat, overtime and tears and, by goodness, she was going to take it all the way to the top.

She kicked off her shoes, loosened her blouse and strode to the kitchen. The cool steel surfaces had appliances strategically placed along them for Tara's convenience. She didn't like a lot of clutter on top. She preferred to look at the clean expanse of stainless steel rather than a muddle.

White cupboards with long steel handles complimented the style. Her steel wall oven and stove-top gave her the illusion she was a master chef in a top-class establishment, and she loved the challenge of making her own restaurant-quality meals.

Tara slid a book off the shelf beneath the breakfast bar, her mind darting to the enigmatic Rick Keene and the strange things that happened in her body when he was around.

She shook off the buzz of sensation. It was nothing.

She flicked through the pages of the cookbook, pressing her lips tightly together. Miss Steel was going to get a kick-arse proposal that she'd rave about for ever—thanks to her father—and a wedding that would be splashed in the papers from one end of the country to the other.

Camelot would be the best in the wedding business!

Tara turned page after page, barely seeing the recipes. What was it going to be like working closely with Rick Keene? This would be her greatest challenge yet. In so many ways…

She slammed down her hand on a recipe—strawberry kisses. That was the one she wanted.

There was nothing quite like cooking—she loved the fact that if you followed a recipe precisely you ended up with the exact meal you set out to make. She wished life were as easy and straightforward.

She opened the fridge and pulled out two eggs and a lemon and reached for her clean white apron.

What a day!

Tara turned on the oven and broke the eggs, separating the yolks with easy grace and tossing them on to the sink. She whisked the egg whites vigorously, trying to just think about the little meringues she was making and not about Patrick Keene.

He was annoying.

She didn't usually dwell on clients. She didn't need to. But Keene was in a class all of his own. It wasn't so much the fact that he'd initially resisted her services then amazingly changed his mind, but more that he appeared to be what every woman was looking for in a man, what *she* wanted in a man.

She pulled the mixer out of the bowl. So, he was tall, handsome and had a way about him that stirred something deep inside her. It meant nothing. He was business. And if she looked hard enough she'd find he was just as big a lying jerk as the next man. Or the last one.

Tara glanced at the front door. David had walked through it almost a year ago. What had he said he was going for? A woman who didn't have walls. Good luck to him. She swallowed the lump in her throat. It wasn't as if it mattered. She was used to men walking out of her door.

She turned away, looking around her apartment. She liked her clean, white walls, her polished timber floors and her vibrant, colourful artworks that she'd spent the last five years collecting. And she liked her quiet, silent rooms.

She was fine on her own. She flicked the switch and watched the egg whites spin around the bowl again.

The business needed her. Her family needed her. She couldn't afford to let her hormones override sense like her younger sister, Riana, had.

Camelot was her baby and her life. It was the one thing she could rely on. The one thing that they all could rely on to be there for them, giving them security and the comfort of family working together, for each other.

She was going to get the job done and get him out of her mind. No problem.

Soft peaks formed on the egg whites. She turned off the mixer and cast a look over the instructions again. She just needed to relax, that was all. She was too tense. The recipe was a simple one, and just what she needed.

Kasey Steel was lucky having a father so devoted to her. She weighed out the sugar and squeezed a lemon. He was there for her. He loved her so much that he wanted everything in her life to be perfect.

Everything she didn't have.

Tara slowly added the sugar and lemon juice, flicking the mixer on and watching the sugar dissolve. She hadn't seen her own father since she was thirteen, when he'd gone out to get some milk and hadn't come back.

Her mother didn't speak about him much at all, as though it was normal for a man to take that long getting milk.

Mum never seemed to worry whether there was something she could have done to make him stay, make him still love them. Like Tara did.

She sighed. Finally finding out the truth had been hard, even at eighteen, that her father had left them for a blonde bombshell and had gone to some European country, leaving them behind, forgetting all about them as though they were nothing more than old clothes he hadn't wanted to wear any more.

She would've liked a father like Mr Steel—the perfect dad. Kind, considerate and ever watchful of her happiness. Protecting her and the family from the harsh realities of life, instead of the realities being dumped firmly and squarely on her own shoulders.

Although Mr Steel may be taking things a little far with his pushiness with Rick and Kasey.

Tara stared at the bench and cringed. The eggshells were half on the sink, half on the bench, the remnants splattered across the surface amid the sugar that had flooded from the packet. The lemon rinds and squeezer had made a puddle of their own.

She grabbed the sponge and wiped up the mess she'd created on the clean steel bench. She had to keep control. Stay calm and do her job. No problem at all.

The phone rang.

'Tara, honey, I've been thinking,' her mother's voice chimed. 'A couple called this afternoon wanting to see us about planning their wedding.'

Tara juggled the phone, rinsing the sponge. 'That's what we do.'

'The Colsens want their wedding in six weeks.'

She wiped the surface again. 'That's not impossible. I'm not near my computer but you'd know what you two have got on.'

There was a long pause. 'I think it'd be great if you could take this one on.'

Tara's heart jolted. 'On my own? As a wedding planner?'

'Sure. You organise everything else for us. There's no reason that you can't do it. It just takes a bit of time and patience to deal with the clients.'

Tara wiped the bench again for good measure and flung the sponge into the sink. 'Of course, I could do that.'

'I was thinking that Maggie could take on more of what you've been doing,' her mother said carefully.

Tara's stomach tightened. 'I don't know…it's a lot of responsibility looking after the entire office, the books and the orders.'

'You think about it, honey. It's about time you moved on to bigger things.'

Tara smiled. 'Absolutely.'

'You haven't got anything else on, have you? It's going to be pretty full on to organise the wedding in that sort of time frame.'

She wiped her hands on her apron. 'I've got one proposal to plan and that's it.' And Rick Keene wouldn't take long at all, being a successful businessman used to making quick decisions. 'And Mr Faulkner, my regular Thursday, who's almost ready to propose.'

'Great.'

Tara rang off, smiling. What a wonderful opportunity…everything she had dreamed of…now they were truly all doing it together.

She opened a drawer and pulled out the piping bag. In no time at all she'd have him out of her life, out of her mind and on to bigger and brighter things.

She spooned the mixture into the bag and piped small rosettes of the mixture on to a foil covered baking tray.

Tara slid the tray in the oven, scanning the instructions for the strawberry cream to go with them.

In just a few more days she'd have everything she could ever want. Right after she got Rick Keene out of the way.

CHAPTER SEVEN

TARA stood stock still, her hand still on the door handle, staring into Rick Keene's office. Her stomach was tight, her breath heavy, her legs shaky at the thought of entering the man's lair.

He sat in his large leather chair as though he were a king on a throne. His Armani suit was dark, shaping his shoulders and wide chest to perfection. His shirt was caramel and his tie a metallic bronze.

Her weekend had been filled with thoughts of the man, and now here he was, in the flesh.

Rick beckoned her in, a phone in his other hand.

She forced her legs into motion, sauntering into the large expanse of an office with as much of her cool calm as she could collect. She could do this.

He finished the call and hung up. 'Sorry about that. I'm flat out juggling work with…all this.'

'I know what you mean.' She sat down in the chair opposite his desk, crossing her legs and placing her folder across her lap. 'It must be difficult for you to relax and forget about your company.'

'It is.' He ran his gaze over her boldly. 'The only way I can get my mind off work is to take on sports that I have to focus on one hundred percent.'

Tara glanced out the full height windows, struggling

to maintain her composure and her pulse. It was just a male thing… nothing to worry about. She let her gaze wander back to the man. 'I know.'

He lifted an eyebrow. 'You know?'

'I mean… I know what you mean.' Her cheeks heated annoyingly. The last thing she wanted was for him to think that she'd spent her valuable time looking over old newspapers for mention of him.

His eyes were sharp and assessing. 'I appreciate your coming in.'

She shifted nervously. 'That's okay.' She shouldn't really mind fighting traffic to get here for their appointment. It gave him the extra time to work and his own territory, and Camelot an amazing future. This would be time well spent. 'We're here to please.'

He shot her a look, his eyes glittering.

She ran her hands over the edges of the folder. 'Okay, firstly, do you have any questions?'

He shook his head. 'Not really.'

'Okay.' She tried not to look at him. 'Have you given any thought to the way you'd like to propose?'

Rick leant back in his chair. 'Do I have the freedom to choose anything?'

'Within reason,' she stated calmly. This was territory she could handle. She opened her folder. 'I feel pretty confident that we can organise whatever you'd like.'

He folded his hands over his chest. 'What if I wanted to propose on the ocean floor.'

'Well, we can arrange scuba gear, communication devices, boat hire.'

'And if I wanted to propose on the back of a camel at the foot of the great pyramid of Egypt?'

She couldn't help but smile. 'I'll get in touch with the airlines and book you two a flight, organise your hotel and a camel to meet you there.'

His mouth twitched. 'What about proposing at a castle?'

'Nice idea—very romantic too. There are plenty of castles to choose from in Europe. I can organise a romantic ride in a horse-drawn coach that takes you to the castle where, amidst the stone walls seeped in history, you can make your declaration of love.' She mentally crossed her fingers. It would be an amazing proposal to prepare and could easily mean a trip to Europe for her...

'I wasn't serious.'

Tara pulled back her shoulders. 'I am.'

'I can see that.'

She lifted her chin. '*Where* you choose to go down on one knee and make that declaration of love sets the mood. The words you choose to propose define your love and devotion. And how much trouble you take to make that one little question the most magical moment in your beloved's life will mean a lot to her.'

Rick stared at her.

She looked around the room, avoiding his gaze. She straightened the papers on the folder.

'What things have men said *to you* that were terribly romantic?'

'Me?' She glanced at Rick, her pulse pounding through her like a stampede.

Rick faced her, his neck muscles tense. 'You, Tara. Surely to be such an expert your boyfriend must be a poet.' He could hear the rasp in his voice. He cleared his throat. It wasn't as if he cared whether or not there was a man in her life.

'I don't have a boyfriend.'

'And you're not married?'

'Hence the *miss* at the start of my name,' she said defensively.

He leant back in his seat, crossing his legs at his ankles, throwing his chest out against his crossed arms.

He raised an eyebrow. Was she as drawn to him as he was to her? There was nothing in her demeanour that would suggest so...

'You don't mind me asking, do you?' he asked, watching her. She guarded her thoughts carefully, the only indication in her deep, dark eyes.

She waved him off. 'I'm fine. Not at all.'

'I'm just interested in what qualifies *you* to tell *me* what sort of proposal plan will work for the woman I love and what won't?'

She shot him an irresistibly devastating grin. 'For starters, I'm a woman.'

'Right.' He sucked in a breath. She was full of surprises. He had to smile. She was one hell of a challenge to him, on all fronts. 'Okay. You have me there.'

She played with the pen on her folder, sitting straighter, taller and lifting her chin. 'Secondly, I've been doing this for some time.'

'How long?'

She glanced at the folder in front of her. 'Oh…ages.'

He stared at her wild hair. 'Could we get a time frame here so I feel a little more assured that I'm not just talking to a fly-by-night planner.'

Her dark eyes stabbed him. 'My family has been in the business for over thirteen years.'

He nodded. 'Okay.' He jerked to his feet, thrusting his hands in his pockets and striding to the windows.

'Anything else you'd like to ask?'

He spun round to face her. 'Why do it?'

'Because proposals are special and my mission is to help men to make their proposals as special and as magical as they should be.'

Rick stared down at her, his mind tumbling around how nice it would be to make something special and magical with Tara Andrews, all night long… if he could chip through her icy armour and get to the woman underneath.

He reduced the distance between them.

Tara met his gaze unflinchingly.

He crossed his arms. 'Are *you* terribly romantic?'

She swallowed hard. 'Pardon?'

'Do you like romance?' he asked, walking slowly past her and back again.

'Doesn't every girl?' she said evenly, looking up at him with cool, dark eyes.

He paced the floor, breathing deep, trying to keep his tone neutral, trying to keep the mood casual. 'I'm asking about *you*.'

She bit her bottom lip. 'What about Kasey?'

Rick stalled. '*What* about Kasey?'

She raised her finely arched eyebrows. 'Well, is she keen on romance? Romantic movies? Flowers? Sweet surprises?'

He crossed his arms over his chest, his blood chilling. 'Why?'

She tapped her pen against her folder. 'To assist you in designing the most romantic proposal plan we need to know what Miss Steel is partial to. There'd be no point setting a table for two on a beach with a lone violinist playing sweet melodies if she hated sand between her toes and couldn't abide classical music. Would there?'

Rick couldn't help but stare at her. 'No—o.' She was amazing—and incredible.

'So, what do you think she'll like?'

He stared down at her, running a hand through his hair. Maybe he should have put some more thought into this before she'd come.

He hadn't considered how much there was to a proposal. It wasn't just dropping to one's knee and popping the question, it was a whole lot more than what it seemed. Like Tara Andrews. And the problem was that he only knew Kasey as well as anyone could know someone who was like a kid sister.

He knew she liked candy, giant stuffed bears and boys. But he didn't think that would sit well with Tara. She was shrewd. And the last thing he needed was her figuring out the truth.

'You've met her…' he suggested.

'She doesn't strike me as the adventurous type.'

Rick shook his head. 'No. So I guess we won't need the parachute or the scuba gear. Have you found many women that adventurous in your time as a planner?'

'There are varying degrees of adventurous. Jogging in quiet areas, riding the train late at night, fighting for a career or to have it all…'

'I get your point.' He ran his gaze over Tara, up her long legs, over her black skirt, white shirt and smooth neck. The tilt on her chin was high, her eyes narrowed and her mouth pulled thin. 'Do you ride the train late at night?'

'No.'

'Jog at night?'

'No.'

Rick watched her carefully. 'Are you fighting for a career and to have—?'

'I'm thinking that Kasey would probably appreciate a quiet place where the two of you can talk and be close,' she said quickly.

He straightened, sobering. Kasey. Right. He had to impose a cast-iron control on himself and keep his mind where it should be and not on Tara Andrews's fine eyes and full lips. 'I think a restaurant would be suitable, upmarket maybe, with soft music?'

She tapped the pen against her lips again. 'Okay.' She nodded, her face brightening. 'Would this restaurant be on this continent?'

He nodded. 'I'm too busy to go far just now.'

'Good busy?' she asked, her voice gentle.

'Yes.'

'Great.' She scribbled on the page in front of her. 'Have you got anywhere in mind? Where you first met maybe?'

Rick shook his head. 'No.' Not a chance. That would have been in the Steels' backyard where Kasey had been playing on the swings.

Tara tapped the pen on her full red lips. 'A favourite place you go to together perhaps?'

He shook his head, watching her mouth, his body warming.

'O—kay.' She snapped her folder closed and stood up, smoothing her skirt over her hips. 'Then I'll arrange for you to visit the top romantic restaurants in the city.'

'Sounds good.' He nodded, struggling to maintain an even tone. Going out with Tara was going to be a delight, and an opportunity to peel some of her damned layers.

'How does tomorrow sound?' she asked casually. 'I could probably organise your visits between two and four.'

He clenched his jaw tight, her words sinking in ominously. 'During the day? Alone?'

'Yes. You could check out the places, the size of the venue, the intimacy of the layout and the appeal of the décor. I could probably arrange for you to talk to the chef and the staff of each restaurant so you get a good idea of what goes on and what gets served.'

He shook his head, throwing out his chest. 'No, I don't think so.'

'Sorry?'

'I want to go in the evening.' He rubbed his jaw, mulling over the possibilities. 'I'd like to see what it would be like on the night. I want to check out the food, the music and the service. We could try them out, one by one.'

'We?' Her voice broke.

'Yes. You and I.' He couldn't help but smile at the perplexed look on her face. 'I don't want to be dragging Kasey from one venue to another—she'd probably get a bit suspicious.'

She nodded slowly, her eyes dark and distant. 'True. Okay.' She strode to the door. 'I'll make the arrangements then for…when are you free?'

He smiled. 'Tomorrow night is good for me.'

'Fine. Okay. I can do that,' she said, her voice cool and steady.

Hell, she was a challenge! Rick watched her standing there, all prim and proper, with her wild hair and passionate convictions. How on earth did she stay so calm and self-assured the entire time?

He clenched his jaw, leaning against his desk and staring down at the woman, pondering what it could possibly take to melt her resistance.

Even in her demure suit she reminded his body of what she'd looked like the other night, of her curves beneath the suit, and all that smooth skin. He rubbed his jaw. God. What was she doing to him?

He shoved his hands in his pockets. 'Tomorrow, then.'

He watched her go, his heart hammering in his chest. He was as skittish as a schoolboy. It wasn't as if she was a date. She was business. *All* business...

He'd have to keep that in mind or risk the lot. His merger and Kasey's trust. And there was no way in hell he'd do that. For anyone. Come hell or high water, no matter how much of a challenge she was.

CHAPTER EIGHT

RICK stood at the bar, his black tailored trousers making the most of his long legs and cute butt. His shirt was lime, stretching across his wide shoulders…the expanse awfully tempting.

Tara paused, her hands itching.

She couldn't believe she was here, doing this, with him. She'd half hoped his secretary wasn't as efficient as she sounded and hadn't passed on the time and place to meet her so she wouldn't have to endure the strange things that happened in her belly when she was near him.

She straightened tall, throwing back her shoulders and lifting her chin, dragging deep slow breaths into her lungs. She'd need all the control she could muster.

Keeping her cool was the key, and keeping her distance. And here he was standing at the bar, all six feet of powerful, perturbing male. At least she knew he was serious about proposing, serious about Kasey, and seriously *not* thinking anything about her.

So he fitted her image of what her dream-man would be like—it was coincidence, that was all. Six feet of tall, dark and handsome wasn't going to put her off doing her job and keeping absolutely and totally professional.

Rick turned as though he'd felt her there staring at his back. 'Tara…you look…good,' he said, his eyes raking her boldly.

'You too.' She couldn't help but notice his freshly shaven face, his hair combed neatly back, and his emerald silk tie shimmering, like his eyes.

The silence lengthened between them.

'Would you like a drink?' he asked.

'I'd love a drink,' Tara replied, slipping on to the bar stool next to him and surveying the room. It was a large bar, dimly lit, with low tables scattered around the room, most occupied.

'What's your poison?' he asked.

'Claret, please.' There were quite a few people milling about the room, nestled in deep chairs with small tables between them laden with nuts, nibbles and glasses.

Tara took a deep, slow breath. Rick's gentle spicy scent filled her nostrils, all sweet and soapy…

'So?' he asked, his voice deep and resonant.

She sat taller. 'So, I have us all set up to run through the restaurants tonight in short sessions.'

'All in one night?'

'I like to be efficient, Rick.' Gawd, did he think that she would consider assessing restaurants with him night after night after night? Keeping her cool, her distance and her thoughts to herself?

'Sure. Of course.' His voice was smooth and deep. 'How'll we play it?'

'Drinks here, entrée at the next, then a meal, dessert and coffee at the next.'

He nodded, his eyes narrowing. 'You are efficient. Great. And here I was thinking we'd be spending days on this.'

She glanced at him, eyeing him carefully. He didn't sound thrilled with the prospect of the quick and efficient assessments.

He took a gulp of his drink. 'Anything else I need to know?'

Tara could only stare at him. Did he have any idea what he was getting into? Did he realise the enormity of the decision he was making—tying himself down to one woman, forsaking all the rest, accepting he'd found the *right* one. *Had he?*

She clasped her hands around her glass, staring into the rich burgundy liquid. 'There are lots of responsibilities for a groom these days.'

'Oh?' He leant an elbow on the bar, giving her his full attention. 'Aren't we jumping the gun a bit? Kasey hasn't said yes yet.'

'Is there any doubt?'

'No—o,' he said slowly, glancing at her with hooded eyes. 'Of course not. Unless I totally muck up the proposal.'

She sipped her wine, savouring the cool, rich flavour, buying herself some time. Was Rick insecure? She hardly thought it could be possible. 'You'll be fine… with my help. As long as you avoid any mention of balls-and-chains, the jail sentence or referring in any way to her winning and you begrudgingly admitting defeat.'

'I'll do my best.' He shot her a boyish grin.

Awareness surged through her body. 'I hope so,' she managed, straightening the coaster to line up with the base of her glass.

She couldn't help but look at him. Had he seen her reaction? She hoped not. Heat infused her cheeks at the thought.

Rick's emerald green gaze was on her, deep and dark and dangerously intent. He jerked to his feet. 'How about we go and see what they've got to offer here?'

Tara took one last gulp of the wine, standing up. She took a deep, slow breath. 'Unless you're considering proposing in the bar,' she joked, trying to lighten the mood between them.

'No.' He gestured to the entrance to the dining area, his hand poised close to hers, his eyes avoiding hers. 'That wasn't what I was thinking.'

Tara forced herself to move, biting down on her response. The last thing she wanted was to know what he was thinking…

'Looks like a popular place.' Rick stepped into the foyer of the second restaurant, allowing his eyes to adjust to the soft light. He couldn't help but look at her, admire her, and be intrigued by her cool and calm control.

Her black suit and crisp white shirt couldn't disguise the passion that he was sure lay hidden beneath the conservative façade she wore.

He was almost sure he'd seen a flicker of something in her eyes, in the way she had held her body at the bar…and he was all for digging deeper.

She beckoned him with a finger, the nail smooth, rounded and unvarnished. 'Follow me.'

He weaved after her through the crowd of people milling in the foyer, queuing for a table. She moved so gracefully, so sensuously, that he was sure she was hiding a vibrant woman beneath the surface. And he couldn't wait to get to know her better.

'Tara,' the *maître d'* said, wrapping her arms around Tara in a bear hug. 'I haven't seen you in ages.'

'No, I've been busy,' Tara said warmly to the large woman, a soft smile on her face.

Rick shoved his hands into his trouser pockets. What he would give for her to look at him that way…

'So is this a social visit or a business one?' The older woman eyed him up and down and shot Tara an exaggerated wink.

'Business,' Tara said stiffly. 'A quickie. Just the entrée.'

'So you're thinking of proposing?' the *maître d'* said to him, her eyebrows rising fractionally.

Rick tugged at his green tie. 'Yes. I am.'

'Are you sure you've got the right woman?' The woman nodded her head towards Tara.

Tara grabbed her arm. 'You're as bad as my mother. Leave him alone. He's totally in love with a beautiful young woman.'

Rick sobered. Kasey. And Kasey and his supposed

relationship with her had to take priority over peeling Miss Tara Andrews's layers.

He followed the two women to an intimate table in the far corner of the room, quashing his disappointment.

The *maître d'* waited for them to sit. 'This is far enough away from the pianist to whisper sweet nothings to each other, yet public enough for lovers not to get all primal.'

'Get back to work,' Tara ordered, a smile on her face.

Rick watched the woman leave, looking around him. She was right. The table was perfect. Almost alone, yet not.

He glanced at Tara, straightening her napkin on her lap, and the setting in front of her, and the vase.

Hmm. Sweet nothings… He could almost see himself leaning over, close to Tara's smooth neck, breathing in her sweet perfume, whispering sweet nothings in her ear, pressing his lips against her skin, against her cheek, and down to her lips.

'Do you like it so far?'

He nodded, quelling the heat coursing through him. This wasn't the time, or the place. 'Your mother does a bit of matchmaking, does she?' he blurted, gesturing toward the *maître d'* leaving their table.

'I'm sorry about that. It's the business.' She aligned the cutlery, adjusting their position until they were equal distances from the edge of the table. 'Everyone expects you…to be romantically involved.'

'I can see that. So, why aren't you?'

'I don't have time.' She straightened her napkin on

her lap again. 'I brought my sisters and mother together under the one roof in business by convincing them we'll go far together, and I'm determined to see it become a reality. It's my dream, and I don't have time for much else.'

'I know what you mean.' Until this business with Kasey he was flat out keeping a relationship going for more than a couple of weeks. The women who had passed through his life had wanted priority over his business...and that was never going to happen.

'Your company is doing very well, I hear.'

Rick nodded and picked up the menu. 'I'm looking at a merger at the moment with one of the most successful sportswear companies in Australia.'

She smiled warmly. 'That's wonderful. Congratulations. That will be a great opportunity for the retailers to buy everything from you—the clothes and the sports equipment.' She took a sip of water from her glass. 'I heard you started out quite small?'

Rick flicked the pages on the menu while his eyes stayed on her, drinking in her sweet voice and trying to discern the layers. Was she interested or just being polite? 'My grandfather left me a large sum of money and his company after he passed away. I expanded it, applying the latest innovations and rising to the challenge.'

'Sounds like you succeeded.'

'Yes.' Rick swallowed hard. How had that slipped out? He didn't talk to anyone about his business, especially something as important and indefinite as the

merger. And he never spoke about his grandfather...
'You do wedding planning?' he blurted.

She propped her menu open in front of her. 'My youngest sister designs the wedding gowns. My mother and my other sister do the wedding planning. I have yet to have my first client on that front.'

'Older or younger sisters?'

'Both younger. I'm the oldest,' Tara said smoothly.

'Are you ready to order?' the waiter asked dryly.

Rick was startled. He looked down at his menu and scanned the page. Food was the last thing on his mind.

'I'll have the soup of the day,' Tara said easily. 'And my associate here will have—'

'The same.' Rick shot her a look, the corners of his mouth twitching. Associate? Interesting word choice. 'So what *is* going on here?'

'I don't know what you mean.' She took a sip from her glass of water. 'You're my client; I'm showing you the ropes.'

'And the fact that you like to be in complete control of everything...'

She shook her head, staring at the petals on the roses in the vase between them.

Rick clenched his fists by his sides. Damn. The last thing he wanted was her to put up more walls between them.

'So, it's a family affair?' Rick mentally crossed his fingers hoping she'd go with the change of subject. 'Are both your parents involved in the business?'

'No.' She shook her head. 'It's my mother's business.

Started after my father left her, thirteen years ago.' She clenched her hands in front of her, plying them together.

'That would have been tough on all of you,' he offered, his chest tight. Is that why she'd built her walls?

Tara nodded, taking a sip of her water as though she was trying to get rid of the bad taste in her mouth. She re-positioned her glass beside her setting, running her hands down the cutlery. 'So, you work a lot?'

Rick broke some of his bread and buttered it. 'Yes. I love it. And I want to ensure a secure financial future for my family.'

Tara froze, her eyes wide. 'You have a family?'

'Doesn't everyone? I don't have any brothers or sisters, but I have a mother and a father and several cousins and uncles and aunts. And I still have one grandpa left.' He watched her carefully. What was going through her head?

She let out a breath. 'Sorry. I thought you meant you had kids.'

He crossed his arms over his chest and stared out of the window at the city lights. Kids, he wished. One day. Some day. He wanted to settle down with a wonderful woman and make a family of his own. 'That would involve a relationship. I don't have time for those.'

'You have time for Kasey.'

He took a sharp breath. 'Yes. Of course. She's the exception.' Dammit. She'd nearly had him there. He'd totally got lost in her sweet eyes and soft voice for a minute…

Tara narrowed her gaze. 'So what do your parents do, and your cousins and everyone?'

'You're trying to cover a lot of ground there. Two of my cousins work for me. One's at university and there's another doing her last year at high school.'

'And you support them?' she blurted.

He shrugged. 'I help them when I can. When I was growing up we didn't have a lot. What my parents had, they shared with their siblings. What my aunts and uncles had they shared with us. Hand-me-downs, bikes, toys…and they bought bulk food at discount and shared in the savings. Sort of like what I'm doing in business now.'

'That's wonderful.' She leant her arms on the table. 'They're very lucky to have you.'

Rick took a gulp of his drink. 'I'm lucky to have them.'

Tara rested her chin on the backs of her hands, her elbows on the table. 'And your parents?'

He paused. 'My Mum and Dad are fine, living in a house on the beach up the coast. Dad retired five years ago in poor health so they're pretty much spending their time together, working out new ways to get under each other's skin.'

Tara nodded, a smile tugging at the corners of her mouth. 'A love-hate type relationship, I take it?'

'Absolutely. They drive me mad.' He shrugged. They'd love Tara's strength, her soft voice and her pretty face. 'I try to see them a couple of times a month minimum, but it's hard to find the time.'

The waiter arrived and served the soup.

Tara took a mouthful. 'Hmm, this is superb.' She looked up at the waiter serving Rick. 'Is the soup-base champagne?'

'Yes, madam. You are a chef?'

'I dabble.'

Rick leant forward, balancing his spoon above his bowl. 'You surprise me. I would never have picked you for the homely type.' Another thing she'd been hiding very efficiently from him.

'I'm sorry to shock you, but there is more to me than all this planning stuff, you know,' she blurted. 'I love lots of things but most of all I love to cook; it helps me unwind.'

Rick straightened. 'Don't apologise. I think it's wonderful that you can balance a demanding career with a beautiful art like cooking.' The woman was truly an amazing, surprising mystery. Unwrapping her treasures would be better than Christmas.

Tara pressed her lips together. 'You don't have to say that.' She took some more soup into her mouth. 'You don't even know if I'm any good at it or not.'

'I want to.' Rick shot her a grin, lifting his spoon to his mouth. 'You'll have to bring me something to taste of yours some time.'

'You're just being polite,' she said quietly, glancing up at him coyly.

'No, I'm being honest,' he said softly. Another layer of Tara's?

She nodded. 'And I hear honesty is one of your strong points.'

Rick watched her, his mind tossing around the uneasy feeling deep in his chest. 'I need to ask you a question,' he said slowly, a vague hint of disapproval coming through in his voice. 'How do you know so much about me? You said you knew I liked sport, knew my business was going well and that I manufacture sporting goods, and knew I'm an only child.'

Tara lay her spoon in the empty bowl, her face cool and calm. 'Shall we go?' she asked evenly.

Rick put down his spoon, staring at the woman, his chest tightening. What was going on? Had Steel given her a file on him or had she been doing some investigating on her own? Did she suspect that his relationship with Kasey was a sham?

Hell. He'd blurted out more of his personal details in the last half-hour than he'd done in a decade. What had got into him? He liked keeping his cards close to his chest, not brandishing them around like a schoolboy for a pat on the back.

Who was peeling whose layers here? Rick put down his spoon in his bowl. 'You didn't answer me.'

She chewed her bottom lip, her cheekbones flushing. 'I happened to find a few old articles here and there on you.'

Rick leant forward. 'You read up on me. Why?' The warm rush of excitement lurched through him.

Tara straightened the dishes in front of her. 'It was a

lovely soup. Wasn't that nice? I think the chefs here are excellent, don't you?'

'That's not what I asked.'

She shrugged, looking across to the door. 'I like to be aware of my clients' backgrounds. It helps me assess their needs for the proposal.'

'Right.' He took the last mouthful of bread, chewing slowly, mulling over the woman, the past couple of hours and how the hell she'd wormed her way under his defences.

He could take her answer at face-value, but he hadn't got this far in business without good reason. If he didn't know better, Tara was more interested in him as a client than she should be.

Her need to fulfil her dream for Camelot was one explanation…

Tara lay her napkin on the table, avoiding meeting his eyes. 'The bill is all taken care of.'

He smiled. 'You mean it'll be on your bill to me?'

'Absolutely,' she lilted, her mouth curving into an unconscious smile.

His gut contracted, his blood racing hot and ready through his veins. If she were any other woman, any other time, he would have swept her off her feet and into his bed without a hesitation. Here, now, he was hopelessly tied into knots. 'You should do that more often.'

She glanced at him. 'Pay the bill?'

'Smile.'

Tara averted her eyes and jerked to her feet. She rearranged the napkin beside her bowl. 'We'd better go or we'll be late for the next venue.'

'That would be a crime.' Rick watched her smooth out the fabric of her trousers over her curves, his body hot and tense.

He stalked to the front door, vividly aware of Tara in front of him. The crime would be if he let himself get any closer to the woman. Peeling *her* layers was fine, but he couldn't afford to let down his guard for a moment. If she realised the truth it would be a disaster. For Kasey and for him.

CHAPTER NINE

THIS was hell on earth. She couldn't keep up this polite detachment much longer. He was driving her mad with his deep velvet voice and his green eyes. And that smile!

Tara strode into the next restaurant, her head held high, trying to keep her mind on Camelot and not what the man stirred inside her. She didn't want all this chatter, she just wanted to do her job and keep her cool, calm, controlled distance from everything, and everyone.

So, the man was a great son and family man—fancy looking out for all his relatives like that. So, she'd blurted out about her father leaving—lots of people had divorced parents. So, she'd read up about the man—she'd saved herself with quick thinking there.

She was not going to fall for Rick Keene, no matter how he made her feel!

The hell of it was that running away wasn't an option. In the past she'd always backed off, evaded or detached herself from the male in question. This time she didn't have a choice.

Tara was not going to back down from this challenge.

She paused at the entrance, waiting for the *maître d'*. The air was heavy with the aroma of the meals, with the chatter of people, with Rick's presence close behind her and the faintest hint of his spicy cologne.

'You said there was lots for a groom to do,' he said softly. 'What and why? I'm eager to be involved, and all, but—'

She turned to face him. Work questions she could manage. 'If you hire a wedding planner there's far less pressure on both the bride and groom, and their families. A wedding planner takes care of flowers, photographers, the venues, the cars, the clothes and much more.'

He raised an eyebrow. 'Sounds like a pitch?'

She took a breath, her stomach tight. 'Because it was.'

'Are you *that* concerned about Camelot?'

She sighed. 'Yes. I am. I'm responsible. It was my idea to get my family together, supporting each other. I'm the one that convinced the others to move to our offices, and to advertise, and that branching out into proposals was a good thing.'

'And you'd like to prove it,' he said gently.

Tara met his steady gaze. 'I want to prove I did the right thing.' She didn't want to consider that she'd made life worse for them all by bringing them together, throwing them all in one big sinking basket.

Rick looked down at her. 'Prove it to yourself or your family?'

Tara lifted her chin. 'Both,' she said coolly, fighting off the swirling mass of emotions. She desperately needed to know she had done the right thing for them all.

A muscle quivered in his jaw. 'And pay the bills by the sounds.'

'Yes.' Tara bit her bottom lip, hugging her handbag tightly to her body. 'Moving to the offices and advertising *was* expensive. But we'll manage. We're managing. We're fine.' She clamped her mouth closed.

The *maître d'* swept up to the entrance. 'You have a booking?'

'Andrews,' she stated flatly, trying not to reveal the pleasure in getting the booking. The place was usually booked weeks in advance but she'd pulled strings left, right and centre and got them in. Dropping Miss Steel's name went a long way too—having an heiress proposed to in your restaurant would prove far better for business than spending thousands in advertising.

The man ticked them off his list with a flourish. 'This way.'

Tara followed the man to a table in the corner and took a seat, flipping out the napkin and laying it carefully across her lap, trying not to think about Rick's barb about her controlling tendencies. She lifted her chin. There was nothing wrong with being in control. She was a professional, after all.

He handed them menus and a wine list, beckoning a waiter. 'Enjoy your meal.'

The waiter stood to attention by the table.

Rick glanced at the man. 'I think I'll have your steak, medium to well done, with your best red. And the pecan pie with cream and a glass of your dessert wine.'

Tara scanned the menu. 'I'll have the orange chicken with your house white.'

'Do you think it's a good idea to put the ring in the pie, or as a garnish on the cream?' Rick asked smoothly. 'As a surprise.'

Tara glanced at Rick, butterflies fluttering in her belly. *How romantic.* 'Not if she loves dessert,' she blurted. 'Or if there's the chance that as she scoops up her first bite she'll be distracted by your soft smile and beautiful green eyes and choke on the ring.'

Rick leant forward. 'You think I have nice eyes?'

A shiver of desire ran through her. 'Me. No,' she rushed. 'I said *she'll* be distracted, not me.' She looked down at her menu, her cheeks heating. 'I'll have the same for dessert.'

The waiter nodded and left.

'So, how's this venue for you?' she asked tightly. She surveyed the lavish room. It was the finest yet for design and layout. Certainly big enough to make a statement that Kasey would appreciate, lavish enough to woo her, intimate enough, with small tables, to pop the question.

The waiter arrived with the wine.

'Good.' Rick took a sip of his drink and let his gaze wander around the room. 'Nice.'

Tara took a gulp of her white. 'Is that all you have to say? Haven't you got any other comments…? And let's stick to the business at hand.'

He leant back in his seat. 'Can't you relax for more than one minute?'

She put down her glass. 'No. No, I can't. I have a

job to do here and I'm going to do it. No distractions. I'm driven.'

Rick's mouth twitched. 'So, you dream of total world dominance?'

She straightened in her seat. 'In the world of weddings…yes. That would be nice.'

He shook his head, his eyes fixed on her as though he was trying to look into her soul. 'I don't think so. You want to have time for other things too. What about relationships?'

'I have great relationships with my family,' she said smoothly. She was closer to her family than most people were.

He raised his right eyebrow. 'I mean men.'

'Men?' Her cheeks heated annoyingly. Men were the last thing she wanted right now. 'Oh… I don't need men.'

He leant back in his seat. 'Oh, really?'

'Really.' She looked to the far end of the room to where the kitchen was, praying for their meal to arrive so she could shove a heap of food in her mouth and not have to say a word. She shrugged. 'They're not worth all the hassle.'

'I hope you haven't let a bad experience taint your outlook on relationships—'

'*A* bad experience?' Tara grabbed her drink, holding the glass tightly in her hand, pressing her lips together.

'More than one, eh?'

She nodded, offering him a small smile. 'I'm not exactly lucky in love.'

'So you've given up?' he ventured.

Tara opened her mouth, then closed it. What could she say? He wouldn't understand. He had Kasey in his life and no idea what constant disaster trampling over your heart could do to optimism, and hope, and trust.

The waiter arrived with their meal. She stared down at the plate the man placed in front of her. How was she going to eat when her stomach was tied in knots?

'What about if the right man turns up?' Rick asked, twisting his plate around and picking up his knife and fork.

'My soul mate?' she said, her voice breaking. She took another sip of her drink and straightened in her seat.

'Yes. Your soul mate. Would you go for it?'

She shook her head and stabbed the chicken with her knife. 'I wouldn't.'

He tilted his head as though he couldn't make her out. 'Why in hell not?'

She shook her head, poking her chicken with her fork. 'Because, with my track record, my perception of what makes a soul mate has been so off kilter there's no way I could take the risk,' she bit out, heat rising in her body.

'Love is about risks.'

She brandished her fork at him. 'What are you risking with Kasey?'

Rick stared at her. 'Kasey…'

'Yes, the girl you're about to ask to marry you, remember?' she stated dryly, happy to twist the question around on him. How cheeky was he to ask her questions like that?

'Of course I remember Kasey.' He cut his steak and put a piece in his mouth. 'The meal is delicious. How's yours?'

She smirked. 'You're changing the subject.'

Rick took another load on his fork and put it in his mouth, chewing slowly, his eyes on her. 'Kasey and I have risked a lot to be together,' he said finally.

Tara chased her peas around the plate. 'Like what?'

'Like her father.'

She laughed. 'Her father loves you. He's gone out of his way to ensure that you and Kasey have a beautiful proposal.'

Rick put down his implements. 'You need to know… Kasey has a problem with her father.'

Tara shook her head. 'No. It would be amazing to have a father who cared so much about you that he'd do anything to ensure your happiness.'

He stared at his steak. 'There are drawbacks to every situation.'

She nodded. 'For sure. But not to have a father like that.'

Rick's gaze ran over her, his eyes sharp and assessing.

Tara could barely move. Her hand was tight on the fork, her body stiff, and she bit her bottom lip to stave off the rush of emotions through her.

No Father's Day cards and presents. No help fixing

your bike, unblocking the sinks, or someone around to kill the spiders that threatened the sanctity of your bedroom. And nobody there with a strong shoulder to cry on, for you or your mother.

Rick reached over and covered her hand with his. 'I'm sorry you didn't have a father who could give you what you needed.'

His hand was strong, big and warm, infusing her entire arm with a strange prickling heat that spread from where he touched her, up her arm and through her body like fire.

She pulled her hand back, shrugging the sensations off. God, she'd said too much again.

Rick shook his head, carving up his steak. 'It's strange..'

Tara lifted her head. 'What is?'

'That you refuse to accept any man on face value except Mr Steel.'

She shook her head. 'That's not true. I do not.' She tore her fork through her chicken and shoved some of the soft meat into her mouth. Darn him. That was not true.

Rick shrugged and took another mouthful, watching her with his green eyes. 'Just be careful. No one is perfect, no matter how much you may want him to be.'

Tara shifted in her seat, concentrating on her meal and not on his probing eyes and questions. He wasn't right. He was just playing with her. She was as impartial about Mr Steel as she was with any other man. And Mr Thomas Steel was perfect as far as she was concerned.

She put down her knife and fork on her mostly empty plate, her stomach tight. Oh, gawd, oh, damn. She clenched her hands on her lap. She had to stop talking.

The waiter swept over to their table, placing their desserts in front of them, pies adorned with cream and dusted with sugar, the crust golden brown, its filling looking dark and rich.

The silence between them was thick and heavy. Tara stared at her pie, her belly tensing—she'd said too much. Way too much. She could feel Rick's gaze boring into her as though he was staring right into her.

She picked up her fork and took a mouthful of the pie, chewing it slowly, fighting the uncomfortable ache in the pit of her chest. She swallowed hard.

She stiffened. She didn't want his pity. 'I'm better off alone, you know.'

Rick put down his fork on his empty plate. 'Without a father?'

'Without complications.' She dropped her hands to her lap, folding and smoothing the napkin again and again. She'd had enough of this. All she wanted to do was get it over with and get to her room, alone, and sleep, alone, and dream alone.

She'd crossed the line. She knew she had. What had possessed her to rattle on like that was beyond her. He didn't need to know her views on romance and commitment, didn't need to hear about Mr Steel. Didn't need anything to put him off proposing to Kasey and employing Camelot for the wedding. And she didn't need him being nice to her.

What was she saying? She needed to be more positive. So, she'd said too much—he probably hadn't noticed. So, she'd let his questions get to her—it didn't mean she wasn't still the strong and capable professional she prided herself on. So, she'd let down her guard—he probably didn't even care.

She swallowed hard, lifting her chin. Maybe if she got a grip and controlled her tongue and her body she'd get to take care of the big Steel/Keene wedding. She stared at the orchestra at the far end of the room, her stomach quavering. That would be a challenging job…

She shook herself 'You've seen all three restaurants now. Did you enjoy one more than the others?' she asked, her voice tight. 'You didn't say…'

He stared at her, his eyes smouldering. 'I enjoyed being at them all…'

She pushed her dessert away from her and stood up, her heart pounding against her ribs. 'We should look around a bit.'

'Sure.' He rose slowly, not taking his eyes off her. 'Lead on.'

She weaved around the tables, trying to shake off the tingling in her belly, moving past couples leaning closely together talking softly to each other, the light in their eyes bright and warm. 'This restaurant is reputed to be the top spot to pop the question,' she stated, walking to the French doors. 'They have a beautiful garden here.'

She swung the doors wide and stepped out, breathing in the cool spring air. She looked up. 'Not a million stars but at least you can see a few.' She could do her job here and now, and get this whole proposal out of the way, done and over.

'Nice.' Rick couldn't take his eyes off Tara. He'd found out the mystery behind Tara Andrews and the truth behind the woman tore at him. She been afraid of commitment since her father left. And was vulnerable. And off men. And avoiding the possibility of getting hurt again.

Rick wanted to pull her into his arms and hold her and tell her it would all be okay. But couldn't. He had Tara the hot-blooded, open, honest woman in front of him and he couldn't do a dammed thing about it.

She swung her arms wide. 'This feels perfect.' Tara looked out at the garden. 'Light is gently falling on Kasey's face from the fairy lights strung in the garden,' she said, her voice soft and musical.

She closed her eyes. 'A violin is playing ''Love Story'' somewhere out of sight and the sky is filled with a million stars that are twinkling like diamonds on black velvet.'

She was mesmerising. Rick couldn't help but watch her lips as she spoke, his body warming at the look of complete vulnerability she projected standing there with her eyes closed. It was almost as though he could walk over and kiss her, run his hands through her wild black hair and down her smooth neck... and find it was all a dream.

'There's a love seat. Kasey's sitting on it, glancing over to the white linen cloth on the small table to one side of you both. It's all set out with the finest china, champagne glasses, the bottle of Dom Pérignon on ice. And there's a single red rose lying across a plate, it's sweet perfume drifting to where she's sitting, filling her senses.'

Rick leant forward, holding his breath, his blood surging through his body, watching her... How could she come up with such beautiful, romantic ideas when her own life was filled with the pain of loss and abandonment?

She moistened her lips, looking up at him. 'She can feel this is a special moment. A moment that you've put a lot of thought and effort into. And you say—'

'Tara,' he whispered, his blood burning hot in his veins.

'Rick?' Her eyes widened.

The noises from inside receded. The night filled with only them, with a sweet silence, with her breath and his.

He wanted to pull her into his arms, smother her mouth with his and make passionate love with her in such a sweet and beautiful way that all her pain would be wiped away.

The magic they'd make would wipe away the rest of the world. So she didn't think about the men in her past who had hurt her so deeply. Or Kasey, or Steel. And he wouldn't have to think about his company and his promise to Kasey's brother.

Rick sobered, stepping backwards away from her. What was he thinking? 'How about we call it a night and meet tomorrow?'

'What?' She blinked several times.

He changed tack, crossing his arms over his chest. 'You're right. This one is perfect. We don't have to see any more.' He glanced around the garden. 'I really see Kasey being thrilled with it.'

She crossed her arms, her lips pressed tightly together. 'All…all right.'

Rick turned and strode towards the French doors, stepping inside without a backward glance. He couldn't afford to look at her, see the passion that lay hidden in her dark eyes, contemplate her full red lips, or the pain in her life. He'd had all he could take for one night…or he'd want more, much more than he could have.

Rick stalked to the front entrance, the silence thick and heavy, vividly aware of her footsteps behind him. She deserved an explanation…

Rick paused at the kerb and swung to face her, a dozen different explanations on his tongue. 'Understand this— I don't want you to think that I… Kasey and I… I enjoyed your company tonight, but it was…just business.' He shrugged off the lie.

She creased her brow. 'Goodness, no. Of course.' She lifted her chin and pulled back her shoulders. 'Understood. Absolutely. Don't think for a minute that I'm in any way…' She licked her lips. 'I'm a professional. I do this all the time. There's absolutely no connotation at all to—'

He faced the road and stared at the cars passing, fighting the ache in his body, his mind toying with Tara's admiration of Steel and just how far she'd go to please

the guy—daily reports? 'I'd hate for any sort of mis-
understanding to occur. You're a beautiful woman
but—'

'Not a problem.' She straightened her suit. 'At least
you've made a decision on location,' she said coolly.

He pulled at his tie. He hated this. 'I'll see you tomorrow then. Ring my secretary and she'll fit you in.
Don't forget.'

He half wished *she* would. That *he* could. He wished
she'd forget all about this stupid proposal idea to Kasey
Steel and just think about him.

For the first time in his life he'd felt pure unadulter-
ated electricity with a woman. A deep fire that begged
for exploration that there was no way on the planet he
could investigate just now.

He had to keep his distance, try not to think about
her, or how much he wanted her. And hell, he wanted
her, all over, all night long.

CHAPTER TEN

HE THOUGHT she was beautiful?

She touched her lips, her steps faltering, staring up the hallway towards his office. She'd wanted to kiss the guy last night! Unbelievable! She was falling for her own romantic babble.

It had to be all in her head. He had Kasey. There wasn't a chance in the world that he was thinking anything more about her than maybe as a friend or as a dinner companion and his proposal planner. She chewed her bottom lip.

But darn, she'd felt the connection last night vividly. Somehow, on some level they'd become closer, and crossed the line. How, she wasn't sure.

So, she'd enjoyed his company last night. So, he'd been easy to talk to—too easy. She cringed. She'd said things to the guy she hadn't confessed to her own mother. Should that make things so different between them now?

She took a couple of deep breaths. It didn't matter.

They didn't have much time left. Tara stiffened. Rick was only in her life for a short time. He could never be her friend… He was getting married to an heiress and she felt things deep in her body for him that a woman couldn't feel for a man and just stay friends.

She wanted more, much more. So she'd have to find her own honest, arty tie-wearing, strong and challenging man. For now, she would just have to grin and bear his company as best she could without giving away how much he made her feel.

She strode the last few metres and knocked on his door jamb. The door was ajar, almost as though he was welcoming her…

He was bent over the papers on his desk, his fingers on his forehead, his thumb on his jaw, deep in concentration. His soft blue shirt was pushed up at the sleeves and his turquoise tie was loose and askew.

'Hello,' she said slowly, fighting the pull at her innards.

Rick looked up and smiled. 'Hi.'

Her heart skipped a beat and her body warmed. She bit her bottom lip and looked over to the Sydney skyline. Her feelings for him had nothing to do with reason. 'Is it a good time for me to—?'

Rick pulled at his tie, tightening the knot and centring it. 'Absolutely. I've been…I thought it would never… The day seems like it's dragged by.'

She nodded, her breath clogged in her throat. She walked slowly into his office, gripping her folder tightly to her chest, her heart thundering. 'So, I've tentatively arranged your proposal with the restaurant for you,' she rushed, trying to squash the rising heat in her veins. 'And I've arranged the decorations for the back garden as we discussed.' She flung open her folder. 'And here's the suggested menu for the night.'

Tara yanked out the printed menu she'd received earlier by fax from the restaurant, careful to hold the very end so she wouldn't have to touch Rick at all.

She reduced the distance between them.

Rick took the page, glancing at it briefly. 'Looks fine.' He ran his gaze slowly over her, down over her new pink shirt and her white trouser suit to her pink pumps and up again to her face.

Tara's heart banged against her ribs. She felt as if she was fourteen again. She slipped out her pen and bit down on the end. 'So that's it. You're all planned so all you have to do is let me know a few days beforehand and I'll have it all set up for you.' She took a deep breath. 'Then, after your proposal, I'll draft up the final bill.'

Rick stood up. 'Surely there's more to do.'

'Nope. All covered now.' She tried to sound light and casual. She wouldn't have to see him again, wouldn't have to feel this hopeless yearning in her chest when she was near him, or feel the charge of desire coursing through her body at his deep looks. It was all over. This was goodbye. 'Oh, I guess there's flowers,' she blurted. 'What type does she like?'

Rick shrugged. 'Not sure…roses or carnations or maybe those fluffy little white ones.'

Tara pressed her lips together, stifling a smile. 'Roses should suffice.' If she wasn't thinking straight she'd presume he was stalling, or hardly knew the girl, or both. Or was that wishful thinking?

'How about we get out of here?' Rick glanced out of the window. 'It's a glorious day. Feel like a walk?'

Her mind fluttered. Why? He couldn't want to spend time with her. Did he have more questions? 'We could stop into a florist maybe and find out what those fluffy little flowers are.'

He nodded. 'Sounds good.'

Tara stowed her folder in her large bag and strode out the door, acutely aware of Rick Keene's strong presence behind her. Her pulse was racing through her body, her cheeks hot and her stomach tied into knots.

She was going out for a walk with a man who was in love with someone else. She shrugged off the tightness in her chest… This was business—that was all.

The street was busy with people. The grey pavement, the tall concrete buildings and the swarm of suits in the street basked in the warm spring sunshine.

The light touch of Rick's hand on her back was like a hot brand, sending bolts of heat racing through her. 'The nearest florist is that way.' Tara pointed down along the busy street.

'The park has flowers.' Rick gestured across the road to the bushy parkland.

'Sure.'

The path meandered amongst the trees and lavish gardens filled with myriad flowers of all colours and sizes. Older people sat on the benches along the path, kids played on the playground and open areas and couples lay on blankets on the freshly cut grass entwined in each other's arms.

Tara took a couple of deep, slow breaths. 'Busy place.'

Rick loosened his tie and slipped it off, shoving it into his pocket. 'I come here when I need to think.'

'I can see why. It's beautiful.' The garden closest to her was filled with marigolds, with both the large flowers and small, the varieties mixed and planted closely so that it appeared more like one plant than many.

'I knew you'd like it,' Rick said, his eyes dark and unfathomable.

The ball came out of nowhere. Tara put up her hands instinctively and caught it against her chest.

Rick whistled softly. 'Wow, nice catch.'

Tara's cheeks heated, her belly fluttering like a hundred butterflies taking to the wing. She shot Rick a glance. How could one compliment from him do this to her?

'Over here,' a young boy yelled from her left.

Tara smiled and kicked the ball back. He caught it against his chest and the grin on his face was wide.

'And nice kick,' he said with awe and respect.

Tara glanced at Rick. His smile was worth it. A ripple of awareness coursed through her, making every nerve in her body aware of him, of how close he was, of how hot she was.

'You like kids?' The warmth of Rick's smile echoed in his voice.

Tara cast her eyes downward. 'Sure.'

'Thinking of having any?'

She jerked her chin up, meeting his bright eyes. 'At

some point, though I figure I would probably need some male input of some sort.'

'I hear that really makes the difference.' Rick laughed.

His laugh was deep and warm and rich. Tara nodded mutely, pressing her lips together, looking up into Rick's gorgeous green eyes, wanting time to stop so she could stay there for ever, with him.

So what if he was taken…? She cringed. Tara forced herself to turn, to make her legs move.

Silence surrounded them. Tara tried to admire the gardens, the trees, the lawns… It was a perfect place for a wedding or a proposal.

'You like sport?' Rick asked.

Tara nodded. 'Used to.'

'You don't play any now?'

She shook her head. 'I did some yoga once, but it was too slow for me. I do a bit of aerobics now and again but it doesn't thrill me—'

His mouth quirked into a smile. 'I could show you some sports that you'd really love—'

Tara looked away. What was he doing? What was he saying? There was no future for them. Not at all. What about the woman he planned to marry?

Her stomach tightened into a pulsing knot. 'Is that the flower?' She pointed at the garden.

He turned. 'Yes.'

'It's a chrysanthemum. Do you think Kasey would like these on the night you propose to her?' Her voice sounded alien and tight but she had to say it. Had to remind him where he was, who he was with and where his love and loyalty lay. For the business... For him. For them.

'Kasey...' he said vaguely. He looked at his watch, his eyes widening as though he was waking up from a dream. 'I have to get back.'

Tara nodded, watching him stride back the way they'd come without even a backward glance. At least it was over. She had his proposal all sorted out, as well as his priorities. There was no reason why she'd have to deal with Rick Keene again...

Or face the way he made her feel.

Tara Andrews was an amazing woman. He enjoyed her company. It was the first time he'd spent time with a woman without being worried about how she was sizing him up as permanent material, complete with a large mansion in the suburbs and European villas. Because for Tara he wasn't even in the running.

What a time to meet her. But there was always after he and Kasey came clean, and after his merger. Nothing would be a problem then. Taking her in his arms, kissing her, was all a possibility. And he could hardly wait.

Desire burned in his veins like molten lava.

Spending time with her was heaven, and hell, all rolled into one. She was like forbidden fruit being dangled in front of him and there was only so much he could take.

He had to do something.

Kasey needed more time so he'd have to come up with something else for him and Tara to work on…

His body ached. Another meeting with her, with her soft smile and bright eyes, her wild hair and deep red lips and he'd crack.

He couldn't keep doing this. He wasn't a man of steel. He was human. Flesh and boiling blood.

Going away to seal the merger was the best thing for him right now. Put some distance between him and Tara before he did something that he yearned to do, but would regret…

Tara Andrews was too hot to handle.

CHAPTER ELEVEN

TARA stood in the doorway. Why she had accepted Steel's invitation was beyond her. She could have given him a vague update on the phone, keeping it simple, straight-forward and professional.

The fact that Mr Steel refused to accept any excuses probably had something to do with it, though she had to admit that she hadn't fought hard.

She sort of liked being around the perfect father.

She hadn't slept much since the park. She'd run over it a million times in her head. Nothing he'd said was inappropriate. Polite interest, that was all. And those looks…could all have been a figment of her imagination.

Even if Rick Keene had shown any interest there was no way she'd entertain him. He was her client and Camelot needed this plan to go like clockwork, then all her dreams for the business would come true and its financial problems would be solved.

It didn't matter that she was alone. Having someone to walk in the park with and talk to was something she didn't have to have right now. It could wait.

She looked around her. She was a professional. She could handle this. It would have been wonderful to come to these charity events with her own father—

showing her support of him, encouraging him to be involved with charities, helping others.

She smoothed down the lines of her new scarlet gown, acutely aware of the plunging neckline, how thin the straps were on her shoulders and how wicked the slit was up the side of the dress. What had possessed her to buy such a vibrant, sexy dress the other day was beyond her...

'Tara, I'm so glad you could come.' Mr Steel strode towards her, a smug grin on his face. 'You're looking great.'

'Thank you.' She lifted her chin. 'But I'm not sure what I'm doing here exactly.'

'You're here because I'm a very busy man and can't afford to waste my time by coming to you. So tell me how close Patrick is to...a certain proposal?'

Tara raised an eyebrow. 'I'm not at liberty to say. You'd have to ask Rick himself. Client confidentiality and all.'

'Rick,' he echoed, his eyes glittering dangerously. 'Let's ask him then.'

'He's here?' She tensed. She darted a look around the room. Did Steel suspect that she was falling for the guy? She felt the heat rise in her cheeks. Was he throwing them together to lay down the law? To crucify them? Cripes, she hoped not. This wasn't Rick's fault. He was the perfect gentleman. It was hers—and her inability to keep control.

'He *will* be here.' Mr Steel chortled as though he'd made a joke, eyeing her carefully.

She took a deep breath, trying to relax, her mind spin-ning. The last thing she needed right now was to spend any more time with Rick. 'I'd appreciate it if you told me what's going on, Mr Steel?'

'You're a very pretty girl, Tara.'

She stepped backwards, clenching her hands until her nails bit into her palms.

'I'm surprised you're not taken yourself.'

'I'm too busy,' she said evenly. He couldn't know what she was thinking, what she was feeling about Rick? Could he? Even her own mother didn't know and she could sniff out attraction like a bloodhound.

'Here he is now. And with my daughter in tow.'

Tara straightened tall, steeling herself against looking at the man who had turned her body into a mass of tangled sensation.

She turned and met Rick's gaze.

Emerald-green eyes glittered back at her. His mouth was pulled thin and his bearing was stiff. His black shirt made him look dangerous, his black silk tie more so. And from the look on his face his mood matched the clothes.

Tara shifted restlessly as Rick and Kasey closed the distance between them, her heart thundering in her chest.

'Tara, what a surprise to see you again.' Rick's voice was tight.

Mr Steel stepped forward. 'You remember Miss Tara Andrews, don't you, Kasey?'

'Of course.' Kasey shot her a smile and then looked between Rick and her father.

Did she know what was going on? Tara glanced at her red high heels, feeling awfully conspicuous.

'I love your dress.' Kasey swung to Rick. 'Don't you love it, Rick? It's so bright and colourful.'

Rick stared over Tara's head. 'Yes, it's great.'

'Thank you,' Tara said tightly, her cheeks heating. The man was obviously mortified she'd turned up again. So much so he couldn't even look at her.

Kasey wrapped her arm around Rick, shooting a smile at her father. 'Anyone want a drink?'

'Love one, honey. Maybe you can get us all some champagne?' Mr Steel smiled fondly at his daughter.

'Sure.' Kasey sauntered away without a backward glance.

Tara swallowed hard.

'What are you doing here?' Rick bit out.

Tara opened her mouth, staring up into his face, her chest tight at the tone of his voice. 'I was invited.'

'I think I said before that I'd like some notice,' Rick said, his voice low, deep and dangerous. 'I don't like surprises.' He glared at Mr Steel. 'From either of you.'

'I didn't realise you'd be here.' Tara sucked in a deep breath. 'I'm sorry.'

Rick's features softened.

Tara moistened her lips, her mind as wild and lost as her body in Rick's presence.

'I invited her here, of course. I hear that you two are doing really well on the proposal plans.' He eyed them carefully, his eyes narrowed. 'I've planned a party for Saturday for my sixty-fifth birthday.' Steel puffed out his chest, his cheeks flushing. 'And I'd love to announce your engagement to my daughter.'

Tara swallowed hard. That soon? A chill seeped through her body.

Rick tugged at his neckline. 'Sir—' Hell. Propose to Kasey? He'd all but forgotten again that he was meant to be playing the role of a besotted boyfriend. Dammit. Tara was a hazard to clear thinking.

Steel was smiling at Tara as though she was better than chocolate.

His gut knotted. 'I—' Rick started, struggling to find the words.

Steel wrapped an arm around Tara's shoulders and drew her closer. 'How much more work does he need until you've got everything organised for Patrick here to pop the question?'

Tara lifted her chin, glancing towards him, her eyes soft and gentle. 'It's not so much that, but when Rick feels ready—'

Steel clapped his hands. 'What will it take, Patrick? What's left to handle?'

Rick racked his mind, struggling to find another task to delay the inevitable, and Kasey's father and his plans.

'You've done the venue, complete with food, music and specific décor. What else is there?'

'The words,' Rick blurted. 'I want my perfect proposal to be scored into your daughter's heart.'

'Really? Okay. Sure thing,' Steel said lightly, giving Tara's shoulder a hug. 'You can help with that, can't you?'

Tara stared at Steel, her eyes wide. She didn't look at all thrilled with the idea of seeing him again, or helping him find the right words.

Rick's gut tightened.

'Come on.' Steel pulled Rick closer to him, wrapping his arm around his shoulder, bringing him close enough to Tara for him to smell the sweet scent of her perfume. 'Tara here will have you all set and down on your knees, proposing to my little girl by, say, Friday night.'

Tara didn't look at him, concentrating instead on Thomas Steel's bow-tie. That soon? Was Rick in that much of a hurry to marry the girl or was he being pushed into this by Mr Steel?

She glanced at Rick. It was hard to imagine him doing anything he didn't want to do.

'You are available to concentrate on this proposal for the rest of this week, Miss Andrews…Tara?' Steel asked.

Tara nodded. 'Of course. I can put aside everything I'm doing and dedicate all my time to this if necessary, Mr Steel.' There was no way she was going to show any reluctance that might threaten his choice of wedding planner later.

'Thomas, remember?' He shot her a wink, grinning like a schoolboy plotting mischief.

'Thomas.' She smiled. Whatever he was up to, she'd play the game for the future of Camelot, and to prove to herself that she could get over this infatuation with Rick Keene if she set her mind to it, no problem at all.

Rick shot her a dark look. 'Well, as great as that sounds, I won't be available.' His voice carried a ring of finality. 'I'm going interstate first thing tomorrow and won't be back till Friday afternoon.'

She knew it. Rick was going to fight Thomas on this issue. She crossed her fingers. About time.

'Really? A business trip?' Thomas frowned, his bushy eyebrows rising slightly. 'Kasey hasn't said anything to me about you going away.'

'I'm surprised.' Rick pulled at his tie. 'It's been in the pipeline for some time. It's just two days in Brisbane for business.'

'Brisbane is a great place for romance and sunshine, I hear.' Mr Steel shot her a grin. 'There must be plenty of clients of yours wanting information on honeymoon packages up there, or even proposals.'

'Ye—es,' Tara said carefully, a sense of foreboding creeping up her spine.

'Great.' Thomas rubbed his hands together. 'Perfect.'

Rick's mouth was grimly set. 'What's perfect?'

'Tara can fly up, courtesy of me, pop in and give you some help while she does some assessment on the venues up there.'

'What?' Tara squeaked. Go *one thousand kilometres* to help Rick Keene with the words of his proposal? No way. Not a chance. Even going two metres to listen to his sweet words of love for Kasey Steel could be lethal to her rein on her emotions.

'What?' Rick's voice grated harshly.

Steel swung to face Rick. 'You do want to continue with the proposal lessons to give my little girl…the best proposal on the planet?'

Rick hesitated.

Tara swallowed hard. This was it. The moment of truth. Would Rick declare her unfit for the job, because she liked him, or because he liked her?

Her belly fluttered and her heart pounded mercilessly against her ribs. Which would be the end of her career, and Camelot, under the weight of Steel's disapproval. A man like Steel had a lot of influence. The right sort of comments in the social set where he lorded would shoot Camelot to great heights. The wrong comments about planners who couldn't keep themselves in check in the company of men who were well and truly spoken for could crucify them.

Rick nodded. 'Of course I want to give Kasey the best, but—'

Tara stared at Rick, a dull ache in the pit of her belly. He wouldn't even look at her.

She bit her lip. She was a fool to have let her imagination get the better of her. After everything that had happened in the past, she should have known better than to trust herself, or a man.

She had no idea what was going on between her and Rick but one thing was now clear. No matter what his deep looks in her direction meant, they didn't mean he liked her.

'Then it's settled,' Steel stated with calm assurance, a smile tugging at the corners of his mouth.

Rick's eyes met hers disparagingly. 'Surely Tara has other things she has to do?'

Both men turned to her. Tara lifted her chin. 'Not a problem,' she said as calmly as she could manage. 'Camelot is prepared to go that extra mile for their clients. And there are some locations that I could do with scouting out for the business. I do have one client on Thursday, but I'm sure he wouldn't mind moving his appointment time—'

'I'm so glad.' Steel patted Tara's shoulder.

Rick shifted his weight on his feet, glaring at her.

Tara stared at him, meeting his gaze unflinchingly. She turned her attention to Mr Steel. He was incredible. The man was prepared to do absolutely anything for his daughter! But was she? 'Of course, but—'

'I'll compensate you, of course. I want the best for my Kasey.' He shot a dark look towards Rick. 'Nothing but the best for my daughter. She's all I have now.'

Rick stiffened, shooting Tara a veiled look. 'I'll be happy to have your help, Miss Andrews.' He avoided looking at Steel. 'Give my secretary a call and she'll let you know the details of where I'll be, and when.'

Steel clapped him on the shoulder. 'I can do that. I'll make the arrangements for Tara first thing in the morning. After all, she's doing all this for my daughter.' He rubbed his hands together. 'I can't wait to see her face when…you propose to her.'

Tara bristled. 'I can make my own—'

'Tut-tut. No bother at all. I insist,' Steel said. 'I'll arrange everything and let Tara know exactly when your schedule allows for your consultations with her.'

Rick crossed his arms over his chest.

'You look like a right bunch of criminals plotting something devious.' Kasey brandished a tray of glass flutes sporting pink champagne. 'What's going on?'

Rick grasped a glass. 'Just talking.'

'Business stuff,' Thomas said. 'How about a toast?' He lifted his glass. 'To success in our ventures.'

'To success,' they chorused.

Tara took a gulp of the bubbly, the realisation of what had just passed in the last couple of moments seeping into her body.

She'd expected Rick to opt out, to see sense and avoid her at all costs, to run screaming from the reality of her screening the great and mighty company owner's proposal, let alone intruding on his business trip.

She bit her bottom lip. She hadn't expected him to comply.

He was obviously totally and utterly in love with Kasey Steel to put up with her father's interference, the planning, and now an imposed Friday night deadline for his proposal!

What was she going to do? Spending a couple of hours with Rick was one thing. Travelling interstate to give more advice was a totally different dilemma altogether.

Would she survive the challenge?

CHAPTER TWELVE

TARA strode into the kitchenette, her mouth dry and her body stiff. Coffee. She needed coffee. No, she probably needed something much stronger.

She was going to the sunshine state for Rick Keene in just a couple of hours!

She'd tried to fill her mind with work but it wasn't helping. There weren't enough dramas, enough disasters or enough challenges to keep thoughts of Rick Keene from haunting her.

So, she sort of liked a client. It wasn't the end of the world, as long as nothing happened. She just had to make sure she kept her distance from Rick Keene and his charming smile and vibrant ties. It was no big deal.

She strode to the counter and reached for a cup. If only he'd stop looking at her the way he did.

It wasn't as if she'd ever fall into the same stupid trap as the disaster that had nearly ruined Camelot. She wasn't fool enough to fall in love with any client, any-one related to a client, anyone involved with the business at all, ever.

What she felt wasn't love. It was animal attraction, lust, starvation of male company, lunacy.

'I hear that you're taking a few days off,' Skye lilted,

looking up from the newspaper laid out across the table. 'That's unheard of.'

Tara faltered and swung to face her sister. 'How did you know?'

Skye tilted her head and eyed her. 'Maggie.'

Tara chewed her bottom lip. 'I assure the clients absolute privacy, you know. I would appreciate the same courtesy.' She tried to sound serious but couldn't help smiling. With Maggie and her mother around what chance was there of that?

Her sister pushed the long wisps of her dark hair back from her face, shooting her a grin. Her coiffeur was like a uniform that she wore. Every day Skye would come to work with the same hairstyle, the same crisp suits and the same sadness in her eyes.

'She'd better not have told anyone else.' Tara slammed her cup on to the counter. She'd wanted her success with winning over Steel to be a surprise for her family. A wonderful, pleasing surprise. And the last thing they needed to know about was this surprise trip.

Helping a man with the words to a proposal was one challenge. Travelling all that way to listen to Rick's sweet nothings was beyond comprehension. She clenched her teeth, sucking in a long, slow breath. But she'd just have to manage.

'You know Maggie—a model of discretion.' Skye closed her paper and folded it, pushing it to one side. She leant forward, a wicked smile on her face. 'So, who's the lucky guy?'

Tara opened the drawer and took out a spoon. Should

she tell her the truth or avoid being honest as she usually
did. She sighed. 'Well, I have a new client. A Mr
Thomas Steel wants me to help his prospective son-in-
law to propose to his daughter in the most romantic way
we can possibly come up with.'

Skye leant back in her seat, a smile tugging at the
corners of her mouth. 'How are you going to pull that
off when there isn't a romantic bone in your body?'

Tara stiffened. 'There is so, I just keep it well hidden,
that's all.'

'Sure you do,' her sister teased.

Tara cringed. Skye knew better than anyone about
Tara's disasters with men and how they'd affected her.
Tara had never been one to believe in fairytales, or the
idea that some handsome man would ride up and carry
her away from the harsh realities of life.

She believed in something far more real. Soul mates.
And somewhere, out in the big wide world, he was
there, waiting. And although she'd like to feel the same
sort of things with her mystery man as she felt when
Rick looked at her, when he spoke to her in his deep,
velvet-smooth voice, or when he smiled that devilish
smile of his, she wanted his total and utter love. Something Rick could never offer her.

Tara picked up the coffee pot and filled the cup with
the thick, heady brew. 'Anyway, I watch lots of movies
and read a lot. And I have a great imagination.'

'I'll say.'

'I haven't had any dissatisfied customers yet.'

'You've only had three.'

'Well, we all have to start somewhere. And now I have two clients at the same time.' Tara glanced at her sister. She had it easy. She'd been their mother's apprentice from the time she'd finished school. She'd jumped into the planning with Mum, living the dream of making gloriously perfect wedding days for couples all over the country.

Skye finished her cuppa and cradled the empty cup in her hands. 'But what has this to do with your little holiday?'

Tara sat down opposite Skye. 'It's not a holiday. I'm spending the next day and a half scouting out the facilities on the sunshine coast and while I'm there I'm helping my latest client with his proposal.'

'What?'

Tara looked into her cup. 'I know it sounds extreme but it's quite on the level. He wants to propose really soon, but he has all these work commitments. I'm being amply compensated for my time.'

'Tara, you can't be serious. Not after what happened with Riana.'

She gulped some of the coffee. 'Look, it's not the same. When a guy decides to propose to a woman, that's a big step, right?'

'Right.'

Tara gulped some of the coffee. 'He wouldn't do it if his feelings for her weren't strong, right?'

'Right.'

'And he wouldn't be showing any other women interest, right?'

'Right. Unless he had cold feet or was a total lying jerk.'

'Cold feet.' Tara mulled the idea over. It was possible, in theory, but she couldn't exactly imagine Rick with cold feet. He seemed so decisive, so in control of himself and all around him that he wouldn't even consider second thoughts. Or would he?

Tara shivered. 'This guy isn't about to get cold feet. He's a rich, arrogant go-getter who knows exactly what he wants.'

Her sister stared at her. 'That's what I'm afraid of.'

'Skye. I'm the older one here. You can't believe that I would ever, could ever, consider doing anything like that. Sure, he's charming, rich, powerful and quite handsome, but—'

Skye put her elbows on the table and stared into Tara's face, her gaze piercing. 'Oh…my…God. Please don't say that you've fallen for your new client?'

'Of course not. I don't even like the guy…that much.' Tara stared into her coffee, her stomach tingling. There was nothing to like about him—his strength, his ties and his deep green eyes were all plain irritating and so were the feelings he evoked in her.

'I'm not Riana, and I'm not going to risk the family's livelihood.' Tara lifted her chin. She was the one in charge of her emotions and she wasn't going to continue this silly fantasy. 'That won't ever happen again.'

'Of course not.' Skye offered her a soft smile and

patted her arm. 'No. We all learnt from that one. Just be careful, okay.'

Tara stiffened. No matter what happened she wouldn't betray the family's best interests, not for her own. Ever.

She wouldn't let her guard down.

'I have wondered, on and off—' Skye stood up, passing her empty teacup from hand to hand '—whether a pretty woman instructing still-single men in the art of romance is a good idea.'

'Of course it is.' Tara straightened and looked up at her sister. 'It's not a problem.'

'Right.' Skye strode to the sink. She turned on the tap and rinsed her cup. 'I forgot, you're the regular ice queen now.'

'And proud of it.' Skye was just being paranoid. What man in his right mind would sacrifice a relationship with the young and beautiful Kasey Steel?

Her mother breezed into the kitchen. 'That nice man who does the flower deliveries is going to take you out, Tara.'

Skye grinned at her, leaning against the sink.

'Mum!'

'Before you get all upset. Number one, he's tall, blond and nicely filled out.' Her mother nodded, a smile on her lips. 'Secondly, he's single and looking for love. And finally, he's flexible with his hours. He can take you out for a coffee, lunch or for dinner or whatever.'

A cold knot formed in Tara's stomach. 'That's nice, but—'

'I took the liberty of taking his phone number and suggesting that you're free tonight for him to pick you up at eight. That should be enough time for you to finish with everything here and get ready.'

Tara opened her mouth but no words would come. She stared at her beautiful mother, who couldn't help but match-make the world.

It had been her hobby for as long as Tara could remember. Everyone who crossed paths with her mother was in trouble if they weren't already in a relationship.

Tara and her sisters had endured as best they could, but their mother was becoming more insistent these days—as though she heard some clock ticking that no one else could.

The last thing on Tara's mind was a date with a stranger. Sure, she liked men, and eventually wanted a relationship. Just not right now. She didn't have the energy to cope with work and a man in her life, especially with Rick Keene's proposal to finish up.

Rick invaded her thoughts. She clenched her mind shut against him. He was a danger to her senses that she couldn't entertain on any level.

'That's lovely, Mum,' she blurted. 'But I'm already committed.' She glanced at her watch. She had a plane to catch. 'So, I'd better get going.'

'Committed to what?'

'She's got two days of surf, sunshine and male company lined up,' Skye said easily, winking at Tara.

'Really?' Her mother's cheeks flushed.

'Thanks for caring about me, Mum.' She kissed her

mother on the cheek and sauntered out of the door. At least Rick had saved her from *that* embarrassment. Blind dates were the bane of her life, as was her mother's incessant matchmaking.

'It's about time you took a holiday, dear, but is now the time? The Colsens are coming in this afternoon.'

'Darn. I forgot.' Tara's heart was pounding in her ears. Her first wedding to plan all on her own and she was going to miss the opportunity... 'I'm sorry. Everything is booked and organised...I can't. Maybe Skye could take them on?'

'Of course, dear,' her mother said, eyeing her carefully.

Tara paused in the doorway, her chest tight. It had been a great opportunity for her but it was the Rick and Kasey wedding that would make the business, pay all the bills and ensure their future in the wedding planning world. For that, she would sacrifice anything...

She pulled her shoulders back and lifted her chin. Seeing Rick again wasn't going to be a problem. He had Kasey, who was all round perfection, and she had a business to make, and her dream to fulfil.

She slammed her fist into her palm. She had a job to do. And damn it. She was going to do it. No matter what Rick made her feel.

CHAPTER THIRTEEN

THE last thing he should be doing was spending any more time with the woman. But what could he do? He'd not only promised Kasey but he couldn't have their ruse hitting the fan before the merger was concluded.

Rick strode to the taxi at the kerb, resisting the urge to look back at the building he'd come from. To preside over both companies would be an amazing achievement.

He glanced at his watch. Nearly time.

Rick was as hot as the air around him, inside and out.

He should have done his darnedest to fight tooth and nail against Steel to avoid spending more time with Tara, but the lure of danger was irresistible. And Steel formidable and pig-headed.

He gripped his briefcase tightly. He was in deep trouble.

His mind was still scored indelibly with the image of her curves, of her bare shoulders in that hot red dress and the irritating way she leant close to Thomas Steel.

His sleep had been cursed. Images of Tara invading his mind and body, refusing to let go no matter what logic he applied to the situation.

He slipped into the taxi and gave the driver the address of the hotel.

She was so different from the other women he'd known. She had a way about her that spoke directly to his body. She had a sweet voice that washed over him like pure sunlight. And she had cool, controlled layers that he'd delighted in peeling. And he was close. So close to the sensual woman beneath the façade.

Rick stared out the taxi's window. The urge to liberate himself from this situation and be free to explore what it was she stirred in him was torturous.

He was stuck between desire and a hard place. Duty, loyalty and honouring his promise had to come first, then his business.

He ran a hand over his face. He would play the game. And make the best of it.

His meeting with the directors of SportyCo had gone amazingly well. They even seemed keen to merge the companies, although some more negotiation was required before they'd decide to take more time to follow other pursuits and leave him in charge.

Rick alighted at the hotel, his gut tight. Would she be waiting?

Rick strode through the foyer, his briefcase tight in his grip. He half wished the meeting had gone on longer, had been more intense and demanding so he could stop thinking about Tara Andrews.

He glanced at his watch. Three.

A sweet laughter rocked through him.

He veered towards the sound, his heart thudding against his chest.

Tara sat in a deep cushioned chair in the lounge, her short white skirt hugging her thighs, bare skin stretching down to her white heels. Her light purple shirt was simply cut, emphasising the thrust of her breasts. The top buttons were undone and he could see a simple gold chain at her neck. A mobile was at her ear.

Rick's blood heated. 'Tara—'

She looked up, the smile fading from her face. 'Rick.'

Rick flexed his fingers around the handle of his brief-case…

She jerked to her feet. 'Got to go.' She snapped the phone shut. 'It was the office… Skye was just telling me about her…' Her voice faded.

Rick couldn't help but notice the heave of her full breasts, the colour high on her cheekbones, the tension that danced between them, electric and alive.

'How was your meeting?' Tara said easily, her tone cool and professional.

'Great.'

'I'm glad. Were they welcoming of your suggestions for their company?'

He ran a hand through his hair. Who was peeling whose layers? 'Yes and no. They're interested in util-ising my company's resources but aren't convinced about me at the helm.'

'It'll just be a matter of time. Once they realise how accomplished and competent you are…and with your track record—'

And Kasey Steel by his side… 'You're biased.'

She put her hand on her hip, accentuating the beau-tiful curve of her body, and just how short her skirt was and how long and smooth her legs were. 'Oh?'

Rick stared back at her, the urge strong to draw her closer and whisper sweet promises to her, to kiss the smooth skin of her neck, to hold her against him. He balled his fist. 'Yes. You just want to flatter me into a good mood so I'll drop to one knee and propose beautifully first time.'

'Right.' She shot him a soft smile and picked up her folder. 'Where would you like to go?'

He glanced around the bustling foyer. 'My suite would be quiet and private.'

She didn't hesitate. 'Fine.' And strode off towards the bank of lifts.

Rick followed, admiring the sway to her hips and the unflinching control she had now. He would bet his BMW sports that she wasn't feeling as cool or removed as she wanted him to think.

She was in the lift, holding the door.

He stepped inside the confined space and punched his floor number. 'You're in a hurry.'

'You must be busy.'

'Yes.' Rick put his case on the floor and leant back against the wall of the lift, crossing his arms over his chest. 'But I have the rest of the afternoon off just for you...us...to get the proposal sorted out.'

'Yes. Great,' she blurted, her voice light and cheery. 'You've only got a couple of days to go until you pop the big question, but be assured that everything is under control.'

'Yes?'

'I've arranged the back garden of the restaurant to be decorated for Friday night for you. The music will be timed to your arrival with Kasey. The table is all set, as is the array of flowers adorning the vicinity. The Cristal champagne is ordered—a great choice, by the way.'

Rick pulled at his tie, stepping out of the lift as soon as the doors slid open. He strode to his door, his heart pounding in his chest. 'Sounds like I'm all set.'

'Thomas says everything is going well for his birthday party. He says he can't wait to announce your engagement to his—'

'Yes,' Rick said, pushing the door open and striding into the lavish suite. The room was immense, decked out in creams and whites, with gilded mirrors and paintings and a deep plush carpet. 'Make yourself at home.'

Tara swept her bag off her shoulder and dropped it on to the white sofa. She opened the large bag and pulled out her folder.

Rick dropped his bag on the hall stand and wrenched his burgundy tie off. 'Would you like a drink?'

She shook her head, looking around her as though she was lost.

He was half tempted to go to her, wrap her in his arms and tell her it was all going to be okay. But he couldn't.

He had no idea what Kasey needed him to do now. She hadn't called after he'd left the message about this trip…

Rick grabbed a Coke from the bar fridge and dropped on to the sofa. 'So?'

Tara stalked across the floor to the window. 'So, we get down to business.'

'O—kay.' He took a swig of the cold drink, willing

himself to relax and let go. This was just more of the same game. Nothing different. Nothing special.

'Camelot has a wedding planning service, if you're interested in using us for your wedding.' She shot him an encouraging smile. 'If you're happy with us, that is.'

'Yes. I'm happy with you.'

She nodded, biting her lip. She strode across the room to the entertainment unit and swung around, barely glimpsing him before stalking back to the window.

'How about you sit down?'

Tara glared at him. 'Why?'

'So we can get to this proposing stuff.' Rick leant forward in his seat, resting his elbows on his knees.

She strode across to the door and spun back around. 'Now?' Her voice was high and tight.

Rick ran his gaze over her, from the top of her spiky black hair, over her wide eyes and her mouth closed tight, down the curves of her body to where she was wringing her hands together.

She'd lost it.

Tara Andrews was down to her last layer. And all he wanted to do was go and hold her in his arms and tell her it was fine to be wild and reckless. That it was enlivening not to know what the next moment would bring.

'Yes. Of course. Time for your proposal. I didn't come a thousand k's to look at the view.' She moved to the seat opposite him and dropped into it, clenching her hands on her lap.

Rick's gaze was riveted on her face, on the deep and

dark and wild look in her eyes when she glanced at him. She was so disturbing in every way.

Tara jerked to her feet and paced again. 'It might be better if I stand up.'

Rick's heart pounded in his chest like a mating call that had to be answered. Her hips swayed in front of him, her full curves beckoning him to her, her sweet voice echoing through his veins like a drug.

He shook himself.

He was an idiot. This was not the time. The place. Even the woman. She lit his fire, that was all. A relationship was far more than that.

He had to look as though he was about to be a groom. To look as though he was not tortured by Tara's sweet body, her dark eyes and her saucy mouth.

She straightened the flowers on the coffee table, breathing deep and slow. She aligned the magazines in the rack below the surface, still facing him but focusing more on his tie than on his eyes.

'So, you're ready?' she asked, looking down at him.

'As I'll ever be.' He hesitated. Maybe it would be okay to tell her, share their secret with her. She'd understand…? 'Tara, you seem to be quite honest.'

'I try.'

'What I mean is—'

She waved a hand dismissively. 'It's okay. I'll try to be tactful in my criticisms of your idea of romance.'

'That's not—'

'And on your views.' She zipped her mouth. 'I'll keep my opinions to myself. Trust me. I'm here to do the best for you and Kasey, and Mr Steel.'

Could he ask her to do something with her hair, with her lips? Could he tell her not to look at him with those deep, dark eyes of hers? He rubbed his jaw. Hell.

He looked away. He couldn't chance telling her the truth. She was too darned concerned about Steel to take the chance.

She sat down again in the seat opposite him, laying the folder on her lap, pulling out her pen and lifting her chin as though she was ready to take a blow. 'Okay. Propose.'

'What? Now? Just straight out and—'

She tapped her pen on her folder. 'You can do it, Rick. This is the last thing to do before you get down on your knee and propose to the one that you love. Prove to yourself that you're ready and you don't need me.'

He coughed heavily. Hell. As if. She was haunting his dreams and his days. Need her? He ached for her in places he didn't want to think about.

As much as he tried he couldn't rid her from his mind. Need her? She was driving him crazy. And her sitting there, tapping her damned pen against her full red lips was a definite turn on.

'Ah…Will you marry me?' he murmured.

'That's it?' She looked at him, her eyes wide.

He pulled at his shirt, popping the top buttons undone, trying to slow his ragged breathing. He could lose himself in the sweet depths of her eyes.

'Come on, you must have thought about this a bit. After all, you've made the decision to marry this woman. Now all you have to do is ask her.'

His gut tightened. 'Okay—okay. How about, please do me the honour of becoming my wife?'

He glanced at her.

Tara tilted her head. '*Have* you given this *much* thought?'

Rick moved to the sofa. 'I have to say honestly that I haven't given it as much thought as it probably deserves.' He shot her a look. 'I've had a lot on my mind.'

Tara's insides jangled. Not her. He was referring to his merger and Mr Steel and Kasey and all the expectation that would be placed upon him as groom and then husband, then father.

She stiffened, trying not to look at him. She wasn't hearing right, feeling right. She was all topsy-turvy with the madness swirling in her chest.

She looked at him. He wore dark trousers and a sky blue shirt, tailored around his wide shoulders to perfection.

Rick's gaze slid slowly over her, catching hers and holding it. Tension filled the room, the very air around them electrified.

Tara moistened her lips. So Rick Keene pushed her buttons, so she couldn't hide who she really was when she was around him. He was her client, nothing more, and Camelot meant the world to her.

'If you were her…what would make you feel treasured?' he asked carefully, his voice deep and velvet soft. 'What would you want the man in your life to say to you?'

He was close. Too close. She could barely think with his green eyes sparkling like emeralds, beckoning her.

With his wide chest right in front of her, with his strong jaw-line and sexy mouth just a breath away.

She clutched her folder tightly. Why was she letting this guy get to her? He was just another man, but Steel was *not* just any client.

She lifted her chin and dragged in a deep, slow breath. 'I guess…I would want him to look into my eyes and tell me that the world was empty without me in it, that his life was dull without my smile.'

She smiled self-consciously as heat burned her cheeks. 'He'd say that there was no music like my voice saying his name, telling him that I loved him. Because without my love there would be no sunshine, no warmth, no meaning to his life.'

Tara sucked in another breath.

'I like it when you smile,' he said softly.

'I like it when it works.' She held her breath, staring straight into Rick's deep green eyes, her heart pounding mercilessly in her chest.

What had possessed her to be so honest and open with him? A warning voice whispered in her head—she was too close, too friendly and far too vulnerable.

Rick leant closer.

She moistened her lips and swallowed hard, staring into his deep green eyes, waiting…and wanting.

CHAPTER FOURTEEN

HE LEANT forward, dropping to his knees on the floor in front of her, his jaw set, his eyes intent and his face scarily sober.

She looked down at him, her pulse raging through her body. 'It's not usually—'

'You are like…the sunshine. Like the dove—' Rick said softly, looking up into her face with such sincerity that her throat clogged.

Tara sucked in her breath. She'd tell him later about directing his proposal at a chair. By the look on his face, he had enough to worry about.

He ran a hand through his hair, looking up at her. 'I don't know…what to say.'

She leant towards him. She was a professional and could do this. 'Just say it how you feel it. Think of her, the woman who has captured your heart.' Tara swallowed hard. 'And say whatever comes to your mind.'

Rick lifted his head slowly, looking into her face, his deep green eyes intent. 'God, you're so beautiful. You rock my world. You haunt my dreams. You drive me wild—'

Tara's body heated, his words sliding through her like waves of pure delight. She couldn't help but lean closer to him. The improvement was incredible, as though he'd finally tapped into what he was really feeling for his girlfriend, every word laced with emotion.

Her chest ached. She was stupid for having taken herself out of the dating game. If she hadn't she may have met this guy before Miss Steel.

'Be mine…' His voice was deep and husky.

Tara's spine tingled annoyingly but she couldn't tear her gaze away from his. He wasn't meant to be kneeling in front of *her*. He wasn't meant to be saying this to *her*.

Her throat ached. She should tell him to face a wall, an empty chair. She licked her lips but no words would come.

He leant closer to her. 'I love you, I honour and respect you. I want to protect you from harm, to comfort you in times of distress, to grow with you in mind and spirit and to always be open and honest with you. Please…will you marry me?'

He stared up at her with his deep green eyes bright and wide. She could hardly breathe. This wasn't real. The words weren't for her. This was someone else's proposal.

A shadow passed over his features as he moved his hands to either side of her chair, his gaze on her lips. 'Say yes.'

Tara's heart thundered in her chest. 'Yes,' she whispered, keeping her hands tightly in her lap.

He leant closer.

Her breath caught in her throat.

His lips touched hers in a feather-light caress and her

body ignited. It was all she could do to keep her hands in her lap. She wanted more—she wanted to touch him, feel him, love him, *keep* him.

She tasted his lips, the ache deep in her body threatening to engulf her senses.

He responded instantly, claiming her mouth with a savage intensity, a fiery possession that she was intent on meeting.

She slid her arms around him, running her hands along the hard muscles of his back, holding him, breathing him in, tasting him.

'Say yes,' he whispered, drawing her down into his arms and against his hard body.

'Yes,' she sighed, parting her lips and deepening the kiss. 'Yes, yes, yes.'

Hunger swirled deep within her, flaming hot, needing more from him, all of him. She tore his shirt from the confines of his trousers and slipped her hands against the hot flesh of his chest, running her hands along the ripple of muscle.

Rick groaned, pulling her closer to him, running his strong hands over the curves of her body and up again, cupping a breast with his hand.

Desire shot through her. 'Rick,' she whispered, struggling for control. She couldn't do this. Not this.

She pulled back, out of his arms, her body throbbing.

What had she done? 'Good,' she croaked. 'A…a great…effort.' She stood up and strode to the window, dragging deep, cooling breaths of air into her hot body. 'Maybe a little long, but…pretty good.'

Rick cleared his throat. 'Right… That's all…you've got to say?' he asked huskily.

'I think you could do with holding her hand while you're asking.' She swallowed hard. 'That contact would make a big difference.'

What did he think of her, getting carried away like that, encouraging his misdirection of his love for his girlfriend? She was so desperate.

Her cheeks flooded with heat. She couldn't turn and face him like this. God, what an idiot she was for falling for totally the wrong guy.

He was taken, he was in love, and he was never going to be hers.

She bit her lip. She didn't want him anyway. She wanted Camelot to take care of Miss Steel's wedding plans. She straightened taller. She needed it too.

'Tara…' He touched her shoulder and turned her round to face him. 'I—' He cupped her face with his large hands, his eyes blazing with intent.

God, yes.

She could hardly think. What had he done to her? Kissed her! Thoroughly, warmly, movingly kissed her.

Her mind spun.

This shouldn't be happening.

Her heart was pounding so hard in her chest she would swear that it echoed around the room.

He lowered his head and claimed her lips again, gently savouring her, softly caressing her mouth, his thumbs stroking her cheeks—a dreamy, intimate kiss that was to die for.

'What on earth is going on here?'

Tara jerked backwards, her cheeks burning. Who? She turned towards the woman's voice.

Kasey Steel stood in the doorway, an electronic key card in her hand. 'What on…what's *she* doing here?'

'This truly isn't how it looks,' Tara blurted, shooting Rick a quick glance. He was stock still, his brow furrowed, staring silently at Kasey as though words were lost to him.

What had she done? 'I… I'll go.'

Tara snatched up her bag and rushed through the doorway, unable to look the woman he was going to propose to in the eye. What would she be thinking?

She closed the door firmly, lengthening her stride, putting some distance between her and them.

She punched the lift button, trying to still her pounding heart, trying to wipe away the burning in her eyes.

She'd fallen for a man she could never have, and had destroyed her family's future in the process.

CHAPTER FIFTEEN

THE thud of the door closing behind Tara ricocheted through Rick like a bullet. Damn. 'I have to go after her.'

'No, don't.' Kasey held his arm. 'You have some explaining to do first. What on earth was all that? You were kissing the woman.'

Rick ran a hand through his hair, staring at Kasey in her crisp white suit, his mind numb. What was she doing *here*? 'I was.'

'I don't know why I'm surprised, you being you and all, but what in heaven possessed you to kiss the planner?' Kasey propped her hands on her hips and glared at him. 'You're meant to be in love with me, remember?'

He was speechless. 'I—'

She stared at him, her face creasing into a smile. 'You idiot. You're in love, aren't you?'

Rick shook his head, staring at the door. 'Not a chance.'

'It's written all over your face.'

'No way.' Rick ran a hand over his face and down his jaw. He gritted his teeth. He wasn't one to fall in love. Never had been. Woman were wonderful, caring, gentle creatures who could be warm and giving, but that was it.

'Fine.' She put up her hands. 'Whatever. I had no idea when Daddy coerced me to come here and surprise you—he's such a romantic—that I'd find you here with another woman.'

'Your father told you to come?' Rick's gut tightened, the heat in his veins cooling.

'Yes. He wanted me to spend more time with you. He truly thinks that you're going to be popping the question to me, like, any time now.'

'Yes, on Friday night so he can announce it at his party,' he bit out, fury almost choking him. 'Hence he forced me and the planner together here in the middle of my business trip to get your proposal finalised.'

'He knew she was here?'

'Of course he did. And he sent you to find us together in an awkward situation.' Rick ran a hand over his jaw. And right to plan it was awkward all right. Had Steel known how attractive a woman like Tara could be to him, or had he just banked on them being alone in the room together? And on his pride stopping him from confessing the truth to Kasey about getting help with the proposal?

'And I did.' Kasey shook her head, putting her little finger in her mouth, and biting the nail.

Rick glanced at the door. 'I can't imagine what Tara is thinking right now.' His gut knotted. 'She's probably hating me.'

'Good. Let it stay that way until Daddy's birthday.'

He rubbed the muscles in his neck. If only the old bloke wasn't so efficient in getting rid of his daughter's boyfriends. He frowned. 'So, that's it, then.'

'Come on. I can't have Daddy winning. He can't get away with this sort of manipulation.'

'No, but it's not like I'm going to propose to you,' Rick snapped, seething, tortured by the look in Tara's eyes…

'Hell, no.' Kasey rubbed her hands together. 'But we can make him think we're okay until his birthday party when *I* can surprise him with the truth.'

'But what reason could I possibly give you that would stop you from dumping me, if this was all real?' Rick ran a hand through his hair, staring at the door, wishing he could stop Tara, explain to her, take her in his arms and lose himself in her.

'I don't know. You were kissing her, passionately, like there was no tomorrow.'

Hell, yes. There'd only been Tara and him, wrapped in a cocoon of time, tasting each other, holding each other as though there'd be no consequences.

He ached for her anew. Damn. If Kasey hadn't come in he had no idea how it would have ended up—she'd woven her spell and he was all for immersing himself in her magic.

Rick ran a hand through his hair. 'The only thing that'll work will be the truth, as your father sees it.'

'Yes.' Her eyes lit up and she clapped her hands together like a child. 'She's the proposal planner and you were… What were you doing?'

'Practising. I just got carried away, that was all.' He ran a hand through his hair and paced the floor. 'I projected… I thought…I thought she was you.'

Kasey's eyes widened. 'Really?'

'No, but it sounds good.' He pushed his hands deep in his pockets and rocked on his heels.

'Okay. So, you tell me she's a proposal planner and…and I'm touched by your romantic notion, by your commitment to me and, bubbling with anticipation of you actually asking me to marry you… I forgive you.' Kasey tilted her head. 'So, now what?'

'Now.' He glanced at the door. 'I tell Tara that's what happened. Tell her it's all okay between us. That I told you the truth.'

'Okay.' She crossed her legs and waved her hand in the direction of the door. 'But when you get back.'

He dragged in a deep breath. 'Why not now?'

'Apart from it not looking real. Come on, I wouldn't buy your story without a lot of convincing. And hell, we'd have to make up.'

Rick cringed. She was right.

'And second, you're too darned fired up—' she shot him a coy look '—for any sense to come out of your mouth when you're near her. Hell, you may even decide talking is for chumps and make mad passionate love to her,' Kasey lilted, her eyes bright and a smile tugging at her mouth.

Rick opened his mouth to argue. But couldn't. Kasey

was right. He shouldn't be going anywhere near Tara
Andrews...

But how could he stay away?

Tara snuggled deeper under her ivory duvet cover, staring at the deep red feature wall in her bedroom, willing
the power of the colour itself to infuse her. She needed
it.

Somehow she had to drag her sorry self out of bed
and into work before everyone found out what she'd
done. Would it be in the papers, or would she just get
a nasty visit from Mr Steel?

She shook her head, fighting the wave of despair
washing through her body and the fiery sting in her
throat.

How could she have been so stupid to fall for him?
She was an idiot. A bona fide twit for sacrificing everything for a man.

She held her stomach, throwing herself backwards,
staring at the plain white ceiling. And he wasn't just
any man. He wasn't like David—he was another type
of man entirely. Rick was kind and gentle, giving and
loving, artistic and strong, and honest.

She had no idea what exactly had happened yesterday—had he mistaken her for Kasey because he'd been
imagining she was her for the proposal, or had he really
meant to kiss *her*?

It wasn't fair. She turned over, yanking a pillow towards her and covering her head. She was so confused.

Rick couldn't like her more than Kasey...

A sob rose in her throat. She shouldn't have taken on this job. She would've been safe then and her life would have continued to be perfect in every way.

So, not having someone to share her life with could be a factor for her irrational attraction to the man, and Rick Keene's quaint obsession with bright ties, and his gorgeous emerald-green eyes and the way he looked at her.

She tried to smother herself in the pillow, the tearing ache in her chest suffocating her.

She loved him!

The one thing that was fatal in the planning business. And she had to do it.

A raw and primitive grief swept through her.

Tara scrunched the pillow in her fists. This was crazy. She drew a deep breath. She couldn't sacrifice Camelot and her family's welfare for anything, least of all this.

She threw the pillow against the painting on the far wall. Damn it. She sat up, lifted her chin and glared at the window.

What was important was saving Camelot and getting them out of a financial crisis.

What she felt was only temporary anyway. She'd get over Rick Keene as she had got over the men in the past who had stomped through her life and all over her heart.

A chill ran through her, making her shiver.

It didn't matter anyway. Rick would probably turn out just like all the rest of the men in her life, because the one thing she knew from bitter experience was that all men were bastards.

Her throat burned and tears stung her eyes. She could live with the fact that all men were bastards, but could she live with the pain of loving a man she could never have?

CHAPTER SIXTEEN

RICK slammed the door of his car and turned to face the building. Camelot. It didn't look like a castle of dreams, more like a boutique in the north of Sydney that some-one had taken a great deal of care over painting with pure white paint and decorating with gold motif.

He rubbed his neck muscles. He couldn't stay away. Couldn't let her think that she'd messed things up when there was nothing to mess up in the first place.

He stiffened. Just the thought of seeing her heated his blood, excited his body and charged his mind to battle.

He strode up to the front window. The wedding gown in the display was elegant, the embossed stationery, the wedding favours and bouquets of flowers arranged around the centrepiece made for good marketing.

He pushed on the door, half in anticipation, half in dread. Locked. Was he too early? He knocked.

An older woman came to the door. The resemblance to Tara was striking. The dark hair, the olive skin and the dark eyes, although there was a sadness in these eyes he hoped Tara would never know.

Rick stiffened.

'Can I help you?' she asked.

'I'm sorry to have come so early but I was wondering

if I could see Tara Andrews?' Rick pushed his hands
into his trouser pockets. 'Is she here yet?'

She looked him over, a smile playing on her lips as
though she was sizing him up.

'Strictly business, I assure you,' he said evenly. 'I'm
her latest project.'

'Miss Steel's man?'

A chill seeped through his body. 'You could say that.'

'Come in. She'll be glad to see you. She was a bit
upset when she came in earlier. I haven't got more than
two words out of her.' The woman glanced at him. 'And
work always seems to help her out of these moods.'

He rubbed his jaw. 'Oh?' His gut jolted. It was his
fault she was upset. Dammit. This ruse wasn't meant to
hurt anyone.

'She's in the first office on the left. Good luck.'

Rick swallowed hard. 'Why do you say that?'

'I know my daughter.' Her mother smiled. 'She demands a lot from her clients.'

'Yes. I'm finding her very demanding indeed.' Rick
forced himself to move, his heart pounding and his
breath ragged.

He knocked once and strode into her office, pressing
his lips together, squashing the flutter in his gut.

Tara sat behind her desk, her white shirt pressed stiff
with the buttons done up all the way to her neck, her
gaze cool and assessing, her chin high and her eyes
puffy. 'Rick.'

'Tara.' He couldn't help but drink in the sight of her.

He shouldn't have come. He should've rung. He wouldn't have had to see her again at all.

He'd been to the office before but hadn't taken in what it said about her—it was small, chocked with filing cabinets, with a desk and a couple of chairs. It could have been any assistant's office if it wasn't for the décor. Vibrant reds on white. Red carpet with white modern furniture, with a scattering of wedding paraphernalia.

Rick put his hands in his trouser pockets, grasping his car keys and holding them tightly. 'I half expected you not to be…in so early.'

She swung away from the computer screen and faced him. 'Plenty to do here.'

'They coped all right without you?'

'They seem to cope in spite of me.' She jerked to her feet, shooting him a shadowed look as though she'd rather have never seen *him* again.

He stiffened. 'Tara—'

'What are you doing here?' Her voice was cool.

He wandered closer to her desk. 'I came to talk about yesterday…'

She pushed her chair backwards and glanced at her watch. 'Look, I'm so sorry… about putting you on the spot like that…with Kasey,' she floundered, closing her eyes, her face grim. 'It should never have happened.'

Rick clenched his jaw tight. How was he going to tell her?

'Is Kasey okay? Are you and her—?' She looked away, her voice breaking. 'I'm so sorry.'

'No, it's my fault.' He dragged in a deep breath. 'I wanted to explain. I need to explain to you that—'

She turned around and put up her hand. 'No need to be sorry. It's my fault. Usually, it works better if the proposal is directed at a wall, a chair or, better still, a photo of your beloved.'

'Tara, I need to tell—'

She stared at her feet, her shoulders sagging. 'Just tell me that I haven't messed up your life. I'd hate to think that I caused so much misery to everyone involved, especially to Kasey and her father. His enthusiasm to do the best by his daughter shouldn't be compromised— and he's been so thrilled with our progress.'

Rick stiffened, biting down on the anger stirring in him. His hands were tied. 'I told Kasey the truth.' He crossed his arms over his chest. 'I confessed to her that I was getting help to propose.'

'And?' Tara met his gaze, her dark eyes shimmering.

'She was thrilled.' Rick dropped his attention to his shoes. 'We're okay. She thought it was very romantic of me.'

'I'm so glad,' she said softly. 'Thomas will be so happy. He's such a nice man…and a wonderful father. Miss Steel is very lucky.'

'Yes.'

'And she's got you too,' she said more strongly.

He jerked his head up.

Tara met his gaze, a cool mask in place as though she was speaking to a stranger on the street.

'Nice afterthought,' he said lightly.

She nodded. 'I just want to do the right thing for everyone.'

Rick rubbed his neck, his gut tight. He was a heel. There wasn't any justification for her to feel this bad. 'Look, Tara—I need to tell you… She and I are friends. You and I… Kasey and I… I don't love—'

She put up a hand, avoiding his eyes. 'You thought I was Kasey yesterday, that was all. It's very easy for a man to project. ' She pressed her lips together. 'It happens a lot.'

Rick closed the distance between them. 'Aren't you listening to me?'

'No.' She turned away. 'I won't listen. It was a mistake. Go and propose to the woman.'

'To Kasey?'

'Absolutely.' Tara stood behind her desk like it was a barrier, the pain of her words welling up in her throat.

This was it. She pressed her lips tightly together, fighting the sting behind her eyes and the tearing ache in her chest. This was goodbye. 'I'll confirm the arrangements are all in place for tonight.'

He ran a hand through his hair, his jaw set. 'Tara, can you give me any reason at all why I shouldn't be asking Kasey Steel to marry me?'

Tara's breath caught in her throat. What a choice. Her heart or her family's welfare and livelihood? She balled her hands at her sides.

She shook her head, not willing to trust her voice, glancing at him from beneath lowered lashes, drinking in Rick's tall frame one last time—his wide shoulders, his smooth jaw and his soft green eyes that made her toes curl.

Rick nodded solemnly and strode out of her door without a backward glance.

She bit down on the sob rising in her throat, sagging heavily against her desk. 'Goodbye Rick,' she whispered hoarsely.

Tara dropped into her seat and leant her head in her hands, letting the pain wash through her, one merciless wave after another.

He was gone. Out of her life. For ever.

She may have sacrificed the man she loved, but she knew she couldn't trust herself on this one. There were too many disasters with men behind her. She didn't have the heart to have another.

CHAPTER SEVENTEEN

'Now propose. And remember, no shining bodywork this time, Mr Faulkner.'

'No problem.' The young man got down on his knee and stared at the back of the chair. 'Please, would you do me the honour of being able to share your hopes, your dreams and your secrets for as long as we both shall live?'

'Wow, fantastic,' Tara said easily. He'd come a long way. 'But it could be a little ambiguous to her. You'll need to have the ring out and be down on one knee to make your meaning clear.'

'But—'

She put up her hand. 'I know, I said to move away from the clichéd but when something works, it works. Have you got the ring?' And, after experiencing Rick Keene's proposal first hand, it worked all right. But then, with those green eyes on her and with his warm voice telling her how much he cared, it wouldn't have mattered to her what he'd said.

'Sure. I have a ring.' Mr Faulkner pulled it out of his pocket and opened the black velvet box.

The two-carat diamond, nestled into a traditional claw setting, was dazzling. The gold band itself, inlaid with tiny diamonds an impressive addition. 'It's gorgeous. Wow, she's a lucky woman.'

He puffed out his chest. 'I'm a lucky man.'

'Remember that.' She leant forward, her chest hollow, trying not to think of Rick and how in just a few short hours he'd ask Kasey Steel to be his wife. 'Do you think she suspects anything?'

'I don't think so. She's got some issues with her father but I figure once I've told her how much she means to me, we'll be able to sort it all out.'

Tara nodded. She hoped so. The poor guy had put so much work into his proposal it would be a tragedy for the girl to refuse him. 'By the way, where did you find out about my service?'

'An ad in a magazine. It was on my boss's desk.' He picked up his briefcase. 'Am I ready?'

'Absolutely. Don't wait. Go and make all her dreams come true.' She bit her bottom lip, fighting back the burning sensation in her throat. She wasn't going to cry again…no way.

He furrowed his brow. 'You've really helped me a lot, you know.'

'Have I?' She opened the door, breathing deep and slow. She hoped that his girlfriend appreciated the simply beautiful proposal he'd come up with. In a small rowboat, on the lake at the park, with a picnic lunch. But then, if she loved him it wouldn't matter where he asked either. 'I'm so glad. Let me know what happens, won't you, Jack?'

'Sure thing, Miss Andrews.'

'Call me Tara.' She returned Jack Faulkner's smile as he strode out of her door. She envied him the simplicity of his life. He loved someone and wanted her in his life so he was doing something about it.

She stared at the computer screen blankly. Was there a future for her service if women in love didn't care where or how they were proposed to? She flicked the papers in front of her across her desk. Maybe her proposal service was an opportunity for a man to show just how much he cared for the woman in his life.

'Hey.' Skye popped her head around the corner. 'Want a coffee?'

'You're still here?' Skye usually left early.

'Yes. I got caught up in the Colsen plans. So?'

Tara looked up at her sister. 'Sure.'

They walked to the café together, talking about the week's business, each step drumming her guilt deeper into her chest.

Skye had no idea how close they'd come to losing their business because of her. She could imagine the headlines vividly—Proposal Planner Ruins Relationship.

'How did your business trip go?' Skye pushed the café door open. 'You were back early.'

'Fine.' She dearly wanted to ask her sister what she thought, whether she'd made the right decision. If Rick was asking what she thought he was asking—she couldn't even think straight.

She felt hollow inside, like someone had ripped out a part of her and thrown it away.

Tara took a seat at the first empty table. She wasn't used to asking for advice from her sister, or from anyone. There wasn't usually a problem she couldn't handle herself, and there wasn't usually a problem that she wanted to accept she couldn't handle on her own.

'So, what happened?'

Tara stared at her hands on her lap. 'He'll be proposing in just a few hours.'

'Good.' She sounded relieved.

Tara nodded. It was good—for Rick, for Kasey and for Mr Steel. And that was what mattered.

She looked across the small shop, avoiding her sister's prying eyes, her gaze falling on a couple in the corner, wrapped around each other like she'd been with Rick.

Her heart squeezed tight. They were so in love…

Oh, God. She looked again. It was, unmistakably, Kasey Steel nestled in the corner booth of the café, passionately kissing a man.

Tara's heart contracted.

The man's back was all she could see, his dark jacket too young for Rick's style, his hair too sandy to be Rick's hair. His shoulders not as wide, or strong or as powerful.

She knew Rick's physique, his short dark hair and large hands, and this wasn't him.

She looked away. Her belly clenched tight, a gasp escaping her lips.

'What?'

Tara couldn't tear her eyes away. Kasey was plainly

dressed in jeans and blouse, her hair pulled back in a simple ponytail and her makeup almost non-existent. She was obviously dressing down. Obviously incognito. Obviously fooling around on the side and she *was* fooling.

'We have to get out of here,' Tara whispered harshly, her heart pounding against her chest. Poor Rick.

'Why?'

'Because Rick's girlfriend is here.'

'So?'

'She's here with another man!' A cold knot formed in Tara's chest. Rick was about to propose to a two-timing hussy and she was either going to say no, she had someone else, or… 'I've got to go.'

'Where?'

'I don't know. I have to think.' She jerked to her feet, her mind spinning. 'I should tell him.'

Skye put a hand on her arm. '*She'll* tell him.'

Tara shook her head. 'I've just spent the last week with the man, and he's going to put himself out there and propose to her *tonight*.' She dragged her sister out of the café and on to the street. 'I can't let him do that. And what happens if she says yes?'

Skye raised an eyebrow. 'And?'

Tara sighed. 'And I think I love him.'

'I knew it.' Skye grinned.

Tara burst through the café door and into the sunshine. 'He's the most wonderful, gentle, honest man I've ever met.'

Skye gave her a hug. 'Then what are you waiting for?

There aren't many honest men out there. Go tell him.'
She jerked her finger back in the direction of the café.
'He deserves to know.'

Tara strode back to the office, a smile on her face,
her body alive and alert. It could take a bit finding him
if he'd already left work. She glanced at her watch,
pressing her lips together. Four-thirty.

She was an idiot. She should have trusted her heart,
should have taken the plunge and told him how she'd
felt. Maybe he wasn't rushing to propose to the wrong
woman.

Her belly fluttered and her body warmed.

She loved Rick Keene.

She wanted to scream it from the rooftops. But first
she'd have to find him, before he made the biggest mistake of his life.

CHAPTER EIGHTEEN

RICK paced the restaurant, trying to think through the haze of feelings and desires raging inside him.

Tara didn't care.

He'd been a fool to ask her, to tell her the truth, putting his promise to Kasey at risk, but he had to know. The question had throbbed deep in his chest since he'd first touched his lips to hers.

He glanced at his watch. Another hour or so and he'd be able to go home and put all his efforts into forgetting the woman entirely. A woman who could let him marry another wasn't someone he could love. Who would really love him.

He had a small table near the back of the restaurant to keep an eye on proceedings, to make sure everything went okay for Kasey and her man.

Rick took a deep breath. There was no way he could waste what Tara had arranged. And bringing her sweet vision of romance to fruition by getting Kasey to bring the love of her life here made him feel a little better.

He dropped into his seat in the corner, a couple of tables over from where he and Tara had been that Tuesday night. Memories of Tara flooded back to him— Tara's sweet voice, her scent, her full lips, her wild hair and her deep, dark eyes—taunting him.

He wanted to tell Tara that there'd be no fairytale proposal in the back garden of the restaurant, no Kasey in his life, no special person at all for him, but for her. But she hadn't wanted to listen. Didn't want him.

He jerked to his feet, strode to the doors and looked out past the curtaining. The garden was perfect, but it would never see the romantic proposal that she'd envisioned.

He balled his hand and punched his other palm.

She was prepared for him to marry someone else and help him do it. Hell. He glared out through the French doors. It was all he could do to stand in one spot and not break things.

He shouldn't have played with her all week, toyed with her, peeled her layers until he was driven mad with desire for her. He was an idiot. He should have waited. Now—now there was no chance at all.

'No, Rick, don't go out there.' Tara's voice echoed through him.

Rick swung around to face Tara. She was bent double, gasping. His gut tightened. 'What's wrong? What's the matter? Are you hurt?'

She shook her head, straightened and looked up at him. 'Don't propose to Kasey.'

'Why?' Rick held his breath, a warmth spreading through him. She'd changed her mind…?

'Because she's got someone else in her life. I saw him and Kasey in a café,' she said in a rush. 'I'm sorry. So sorry.'

He stared at her, a chill running down his spine. She hadn't come to tell him that she cared…

Tara put her hand on his arm, her dark eyes soft and gentle. 'I know, it's unbelievable. I'm so sorry to tell you, but I thought you ought to know.'

'When did you find out?' he asked dully.

'This afternoon.'

'What took you so long to get here?' Had she finished her work before she'd found a few extra moments to pop in and inform him, out of what, client loyalty?

'I went everywhere.' She looked at the ceiling. 'Your office, your place. Then I ran out of time and I knew you'd be here…and then I got stuck in traffic.'

Rick stepped a little closer to her, his body warming. 'You did?'

'Yes, of course I did.' She bit her lip and looked up at him. 'And I want to tell you that—'

'Tara, what a surprise!'

Tara swung to face Thomas Steel, her chest tight. 'Mr Steel? What are you doing here?'

'Please, call me Thomas. Are you here to see Rick propose?' He lifted his eyebrows towards Rick as though he was fully expecting the man to waltz out the door and drop to his knee.

'No. I'm not,' Tara bit out, lifting her chin. 'I'm here because—'

Mr Steel lifted his bushy eyebrows. 'Because *you* love him.'

She clenched her hands by her sides. How could he know? Did she have it written on her face? 'No.'

She shook her head vehemently, the accusation in his tone was like a death knell to Camelot. 'I've done everything I could to make this a special moment for Kasey and—what are *you* doing here?'

'Well, if you're not here to stop the thing, I'm here to see my daughter before she makes the biggest mistake of her life by agreeing to marry Patrick.'

Rick stepped in front of Tara. 'She's not going to—'

'No?' Mr Steel smirked. 'I have tried to make the girl see sense but will she listen…?'

'So what's all your ''help'' really been about?' Rick bit out. 'If you haven't wanted me to propose to her then what on earth possessed you to get the planner?'

'Honestly—' Mr Steel rubbed his jaw '—I couldn't see you making her happy. I had a wonderful marriage with Kasey's mother and the one thing I know from my years with her was what made us work. What magic we had. And I wanted that for my little girl.'

Rick crossed his arms over his chest. 'And I don't have it?'

'No. So, I started thinking. Number one—I figured the proposal idea would scare you away if there was any reason that you two haven't got serious with your relationship.'

Tara stared at Rick, her stomach fluttering. But Rick did want Kasey, it was Kasey who didn't want Rick…right?

'Number two—by getting you and the planner together who, as far as I'm concerned, seems more your type of woman than my daughter, I figured it might highlight that your match with my daughter wasn't *the* one.'

Tara looked at her hands, her cheeks heating. And he'd done a bang-up job of picking her as being susceptible to a man like Rick Keene.

'And three—I figured at the very extreme I'd get the opportunity to show Kasey your interests lie elsewhere.' Mr Steel shrugged.

Tara jerked her head up, her face hot. 'That's terrible. Awful.' Did he know what had happened in Sydney? Had Kasey told him? 'And interfering.'

Mr Steel straightened his black tie. 'I know. It was wrong. But I couldn't stand by and have her make a mistake like that.'

Rick stared at Mr Steel. 'She should be able to make her own mistakes.'

Mr Steel puffed out his chest. 'Yes, but she's my only child and I want her to be happy. Even if that means treading on a few toes.'

Tara shook her head, the realisation seeping into her. There was no such thing as a perfect father. 'I don't believe this.'

'So where is my girl? And are you going to propose now or face the fact that you don't have what it takes to make her happy?' Steel swept the French doors wide and strode on to the patio.

Tara held her breath. Would Rick still want Kasey?

The garden was lit softly by the fairy lights, the table for two off to one side. Kasey sat on a loveseat near the edge of the garden, a man was on his knee in front of her, offering her something.

Tara's gut clenched tight. It was the man she had seen earlier. She'd recognise that back and sandy hair anywhere and she knew exactly what he was doing.

Mr Steel froze in his tracks. 'What in hell is going on here?'

Kasey smiled at her companion and fell into the man's arms and kissed him. 'Yes, yes… Oh, yes!'

'What on earth…?' Mr Steel growled.

Kasey looked up and smiled, her eyes bright. 'Hey. You wouldn't believe it. Jack's just proposed to me.'

'Jack?' Tara's belly fluttered. The man turned. It was her Thursday Jack. But what was he doing here? Proposing to Kasey Steel…

She was his girlfriend? *He* was the man in the café with her? She turned slowly to Rick, her body stiff with tension. Then who was Rick to her?

'I don't understand.' Tara looked up at Rick, her chest tight. How on earth had Jack Faulkner and Kasey managed to usurp his proposal plan? How on earth had Kasey even known about it? Or Jack? It was meant to be a surprise…

Rick looked down at her, his green eyes soft. 'Tara, I—'

She swung to Kasey. 'You're going to marry Jack? What about Rick? He's been your boyfriend for the last six months. Surely you're not going to just dump him right here, like this…?'

'Miss Andrews?' Jack wrapped his arm around Kasey

and strode towards them, a large smile on his face and his eyes glowing.

'You know the planner?' Kasey asked.

Jack glanced at Kasey. 'She helped me with the proposal.' He turned back to Tara. 'She said yes.'

Tara nodded. 'I heard.'

The young man grinned, stepping back a little so she could clearly see Kasey Steel. Kasey had said yes to Jack? Her body chilled. What on earth did it mean?

Kasey laughed. 'She's your proposal planner too? Wow, what a coincidence. You and Dad chose the same one.'

Jack smiled. 'I saw the magazine on his desk open to the ad…'

'Jack Faulkner?' Mr Steel growled like a caged animal. 'My assistant and *my daughter*? For how long?'

'Over six months, Daddy,' Kasey said, smiling at Jack, her eyes bright. 'And I love him.'

'That's…that's great,' Tara whispered, her throat tight. She had made her own choice but then what was Rick? Free? Was he free to be with her?

Her body warmed all over at the thought of being free to touch Rick Keene, wrap her arms around him, kiss him and love him and call him hers. 'Rick?'

Jack smiled. 'I was awfully concerned about Rick hanging out with my Kasey but it's all worked out for the best. Mr Steel—' he reached out his hand to shake Thomas Steel's '—you have a wonderful daughter.'

'I have.' Mr Steel eyed Jack carefully, as though he was assessing the man anew.

'What?' Tara blurted. Jack knew about Rick? Her mind scrambled to make sense of it.

'Rick was great, wasn't he?' Kasey beamed, stepping forward and embracing Tara. 'And so were you. Without you and my sweet decoy I wouldn't have got this far with Jack. Thanks.'

Tara stared at the woman, her body cooling. 'Decoy?'

Kasey grinned, shooting a look of defiance at her father. 'Thank you for keeping my father right off the scent. We—' she hugged Jack closer to her '—would never have survived.'

Tara stepped backwards, the realisation slicing through her like a knife. 'It was all a lie?' From the moment when she first laid on eyes on Rick Keene to...

Tara covered her mouth.

'Of course,' Kasey said, grinning. 'What did you think? That I'd marry Patrick? Come on, he's not my type at all.'

Tara backed away. She heard the words from a distance, the blood rushing in her ears. She turned to Rick. '*You* lied?'

'So Patrick and Kasey's relationship has been a farce to distract me?' Mr Steel puffed out his chest, a smile tugging at the corner of his mouth. 'How dare you be so presumptuous, young lady?'

Kasey put a hand on her hip. 'Come on, Dad. You're the one who taught me to be so shifty anyway.' She waved a finger at her father. 'And you know damned well that you sent me to Brisbane to find Rick with the planner and break us up.'

'What?' Tara squeaked.

'Don't listen to a word of this… they conspired against me. Lied to me,' Steel said dramatically.

'You're not innocent either, Dad,' Kasey said quickly. 'I know you wouldn't have hired a proposal planner who looked like *her* without good reason, so 'fess up.'

'Fine. I used her,' Steel said easily. 'I couldn't see you and Patrick being happy. I figured a nice young woman who posed a challenge would reawaken his real desires.'

Tara choked on the realisation. They'd *all* used her. She'd gone to the extreme for Rick and Kasey. She'd sacrificed the lot, including her first wedding client, to do right by them. And this was what she got!

'Dad, I'm happy. I love him, truly, really love him.' Kasey stepped forward and hugged her father. 'And don't worry. I wasn't just using Rick. He needed to get the solid reputation that a serious relationship could give him.'

'The merger,' Tara whispered, backing away until she felt the French doors against her back, her body cold and stiff. His business was more important than being honest with her?

Steel wrapped his arm around his daughter, a smile on his face. 'If you're happy, I'm happy too.'

Tara lurched inside the restaurant, her cheeks burning. She'd been had. By them all. And the torment of all the lies, Rick's lies, tore at her heart.

Rick caught her arm. 'I need to speak with you, Tara.'

She spun to face Rick in his dark suit, staring at his sky blue shirt and his navy tie with little silver stars on it. She was so sick of his cute ties, his horrible lies and the pain in her chest... She was free to love the man, but did she want a man like him? 'Men are such lying bastards.'

He moved closer. 'Tara.'

Tara shook her head. 'My father was a liar. I believed him when he said he was getting milk. I trusted him. He meant the world to me. I didn't twig even when I went to the fridge and there was plenty of milk.'

'Your father?'

'You lied to me. Steel lied to me.' She stared at the little stars on his tie as they blurred. He'd shown his colours. He was just like all the rest. 'I really thought you were different...'

'It's not how it seems,' he said softly.

She glared at him. 'It's *exactly* as it seems. You fed me lie after lie after lie and I was so gullible I swallowed every one of them.' She dragged in a deep breath. 'I did all this—' she stretched her arms wide '—for nothing.'

'Not for nothing,' he said softly, reducing the distance between them, his eyes glowing with intent. 'I know you've been hurt in the past, that this has hurt you, but I—'

She shook her head, pulling away from him. 'No. I've heard enough. I've had enough. The picture is all crystal clear. I'm not an idiot. I get it. Okay. I get it.'

Rick shook his head. 'No, you don't. We need to talk. There's so much I need to say.'

'There's *nothing* to say.' She spun on her heel, wrenching her arm from his hold, and strode away from him. She couldn't hear it. Not now.

It would probably all be lies anyway.

She pushed through the people in the foyer, fighting back the tears. So, Rick was another man to wreck havoc on her life, another man to take her heart and break it. Another liar to tear her dreams to pieces.

She should have known better...

CHAPTER NINETEEN

'TARA, is everything okay?' Her mother's dark eyes were wide with concern.

Tara glanced at her mum as she entered the wedding boutique, half tempted to lift her chin, stiffen her stance and brave it on her own. She dropped her shoulders, tears stinging her eyes. She couldn't do it any more. She couldn't be perfect. She couldn't be strong enough for everyone.

'Mum,' she croaked, the word sticking in her throat.

'What is it?' Her mother wrapped an arm around her shoulder and steered her into her office. 'Come and tell me.'

'You're busy,' Tara whispered.

'Nothing important. I just came in this morning to take advantage of a quiet Saturday morning to catch up on a few things.'

Her mother propelled her into her office. Tara liked it there. It was just like the one in the front room of their small house when she was a kid, when life seemed simpler.

'I know, it's that trip you came home early from, isn't it? Don't worry, honey, there's a lovely new chef at the caterers who sounds interested in you.'

'Mum, I'm sorry, no. I can't go out with him. You

have to stop doing this,' she choked, her blood heating. The last thing she needed was *another* man to deal with!

'Mum, I think you ought to stop trying to fix my life and everyone else's and look after your own.'

'Tara—'

'You're beautiful, talented and kind. Get over Dad and go for it. You have a right to be happy too.' The words resonated through Tara.

'You're probably right, honey.' Her mother sat down on her white sofa. 'But I think you're the one who needs some sorting out right now.'

She bit her bottom lip, throwing up her hands. 'I thought I had a client who would make all the difference, but he lied. It was all a lie,' she blurted, fighting the tears. 'It was an elaborate farce to fool the girl's father. I worked my butt off. I didn't take on the Colsen wedding. I...I fell in love with the jerk and denied what I felt, for their sakes, for his sake.'

Her mother nodded, her brow creased. 'There was no engagement?'

'No. There was no anything. Nothing. Rick and Kasey were a lie.'

Her mother patted the seat beside her. 'Come and tell me all about it. I'm sure we can work this out.'

Tara shook her head, the words clogging in her throat. 'No...I can't. Not yet. I need to think...myself, on my own.' She dragged in a deep breath. She shouldn't have come in at all. Work wasn't going to solve anything, not this time. 'I'm going home. If you need me...if anyone needs me, I'll be there.'

'Are you sure, honey? I'm here to listen if you need to talk.'

Tara shook her head. 'Thanks, Mum, but no. You're not who I have to talk to—' And she wasn't ready to face him yet, not by a long shot.

Tara straightened her clothes. She would be brave and strong tomorrow, or the next day. For now, she needed to be alone, and she needed to cry…

Every surface was covered in baked goods, from éclairs and pastries to pies, cakes and roasts. Tara had almost exhausted her pantry and fridge in her effort to shake off the tension in her body.

The benches were covered in flour, sugar and mess and she didn't care. It didn't matter. No matter how much control she had over her life, life came and bit her in the butt.

She punched the dough on the bench. She had a lot of thinking to do before she faced Rick Keene.

How could he have done that to her? She drove her fist into the dough. How did he think he'd get away with it? She flung the dough over and struck it again. He'd better have a darned good reason.

The doorbell chimed.

Tara glared at the door. She didn't want to see anyone, but she couldn't ignore it. It could be her mum, Skye, Riana or Maggie needing her for something. She dabbed her eyes again with the end of her apron and strode to the door.

She flung the door wide, throwing back her shoulders

and lifting her chin, hopefully giving the impression of a strong shoulder to cry on.

Rick stood at the door in a pair of blue denim jeans and a striking black and white shirt covered in squares.

She took a sharp breath. 'How did you know where to find me?' She looked skyward. 'Mum…of course. I should have known. Her and her stupid matchmaking fantasies. I don't know why she does it!'

Rick shrugged. 'Maybe your mother wants to see you happy, just like Steel did for Kasey,' he said softly.

She glared at him. Was her mother her Mr Steel? Someone to care about her future, her life, her happiness? Tears welled in her eyes. *She was.*

'What do you want?' she bit out, fighting the pull of desire. 'To rub it in? Thanks, but I got it the first time.' She swung the door to close it.

Rick put his foot in the way, pushing it open again. 'You didn't get the whole story.'

Her stomach knotted. 'I don't want it,' she croaked.

'I want to tell you.' He pierced her with his emerald-green gaze. 'I'd like you to hear me out without saying a word.'

Tara's insides jangled. She fought the urge to fall into his arms, to wrap her hands around his neck.

So, the arrogant, manipulative businessman had come and found her; it didn't matter. So, she got to deal with him today rather than tomorrow, she was done crying. She lifted her chin. 'Fine.'

She stepped back, letting the door swing wide, flexing

her fists. 'Talk fast. I'm not in the mood for a long speech.'

Rick strode past her into her apartment. 'You're hungry?' He gazed around the room, his eyes wide. 'Or you're catering for a wedding?'

'I…' She looked around her. Had she really made *that* much? She couldn't have—cooking always helped, and that much cooking should have cured anything, but still she felt twisted, tortured and confused. 'Talk.'

Rick slipped his hands into his pockets. 'I need to explain to you that we…that I never set out to hurt you. I was doing a favour for Kasey because her father was sabotaging her relationships whenever they went for more than a couple of months. She'd met Jack, an employee of her father's, and fell in love but didn't want her father to know until they knew what they felt for each other.'

Tara pressed her lips together, fighting the flutter in her belly. 'O—kay.'

'She asked me to do her the favour of pretending to be her latest boyfriend so her father wouldn't chase off Jack.'

'Why?'

'I said no interruptions.' He paced the room. 'Kasey's older brother was my best friend at school.'

'She's an only child.'

'Now,' he said, his voice thick and heavy. 'He died in a car accident while we were in university. I made a promise to be there for Kasey whenever she needed me.'

'And you did. You pretended for her,' she blurted, her hands clenched tightly at her sides.

'Because I'd promised,' he said, his voice smooth and velvet soft.

She bit her bottom lip, her mind struggling for the significance to his words. 'But why didn't you just tell me what was going on?'

Rick shrugged. 'I didn't know you.'

'But you used me.' Tara's chest tightened. Like Steel had, and Kasey had.

Rick nodded, moving closer to her. 'I did, but for all the right reasons. Kasey needed me. I didn't know you. And then I did and, by God, Tara, you showed me much more than how to propose to a woman.' He ran a hand through his hair. 'I need you, Tara.'

She threw out her chest, scrambling to stay firm in the face of his smooth voice, his green eyes and his sweet nothings. She looked at him, her eyes narrowed. 'Well, I don't need a man in my life to be happy.'

Rick leant against the counter, crossing his arms over his chest. 'Surely you'd like someone special to share your life with?'

Thoughts of sharing her life with Rick invaded her mind—of waking up next to him in the morning, of coming home to him at night, of long walks, quiet dinners, fast sports, and of keeping him.

She ached for him, her blood surging through her body with the burning of desire.

She shook off the insanity. He was a liar just like her

father. She wiped her hands on her apron and tilted her chin up. 'I don't need anyone,' she stated coolly.

'I don't believe you.' Rick advanced on her. 'I know you've been hurt in the past but—'

She shook her head, dragging in a deep breath, trying to dispel the deep pain in her chest. 'No buts. No. You have no idea what I went through for you and Kasey. The torture at the thought that *I* was the *other* woman, the one who had feelings for someone that she shouldn't have.'

'You have feelings for me?' he asked softly, moving closer to her, his green eyes glinting.

She stepped backwards. 'She broke up our family, Rick.' She swiped at her cheeks, wiping away the moisture. 'I could never be her.'

'And you weren't. You're not. You did the right thing,' he said gently. 'You didn't say anything, didn't break us up, even though…' he rubbed his jaw '…you were prepared for me to propose to Kasey, until you saw her with Jack.'

Tara threw up her hands. 'And it wasn't even real.'

Rick reduced the distance between them. 'I should have told you. I tried several times…but it wasn't my secret to tell, not really.'

Tara looked away. 'My father didn't tell us what was going on either. He didn't even say goodbye.'

Rick sighed deeply. 'I'm so sorry, Tara. I know that your father hurt you. But you've got to get over him leaving you.'

Tara stiffened, lifting her chin and glaring into Rick's deep green eyes. 'This has nothing to do with him.'

He reached for her, holding her shoulders firmly in his large, warm hands. 'He lied to you, sure, but it's in the past. It's done and over. It's up to you how it affects you now and in the future.'

'But if he loved us—' Tears filled her eyes and she nodded. Rick was right. What happened all those years ago was her father's decision—it was time she made her own.

'I know.' Rick pulled her into his warm arms and held her against his strong body. 'But maybe he couldn't say goodbye because he loved you so much it was all he could do to walk away.'

Tara bit her lip. Maybe Rick was right. Maybe her father hadn't been able to face her, maybe he had felt guilty, maybe he had figured it was best that he didn't call them and disrupt their lives any more than he already had.

Rick stepped back from her and tilted up her chin, looking into her face. '*I* can't walk away from *you*.'

Her heart fluttered and her skin tingled where he held her. 'So you were never going to ask her to marry you?'

'No.' He cupped her face in his hands. 'Never.'

'You don't love her?' she asked tentatively, a warm glow flowing through her.

'Only as the little sister I never had.' Rick ran his thumb over her lips. 'I love someone else entirely.'

'Rick,' she whispered, her heart pounding in her chest as eager and erratic as a spring storm.

He bent his head and kissed her. Slow, drugging kisses that melted away the tension in her, firing her senses to him.

Finally, he pulled back. 'Tara, I'm so sorry you had to get in the middle of it all. It all seemed so harmless... I never meant to hurt you.' He brushed his lips over hers. 'I love you.'

She wrapped her arms around him, hiding her face in his shoulder, trying to just breathe. 'What about Jack and Kasey?'

'They're fine. Steel liked Jack as an employee, now he just has to get to know him as his future son-in-law.'

'What about your precious merger?' she whispered. Kasey, she could understand, but how many of the lies were because of his business and his desire to get ahead?

He waved it off. 'Hasn't happened. But after looking over their operations I think we can collaborate on distribution without relying on a merger.' He brushed his lips over hers. 'But that's not what's important. You are. Have I got a hope in hell of winning your heart?'

'Rick...' She swallowed hard. 'You lied to me and I hate liars.'

'You hate me?' Rick's voice cracked.

She shook her head, her lips pressed tightly together. 'No, but how can we be together if I don't trust you?'

Rick looked down into her face, his green eyes bright with promise. 'Can you learn to trust me?'

She shrugged. 'That'll take time.'

Rick stared down into her face, his green eyes shining

with his love for her. 'I'm prepared to take all the time in the world.'

His mouth moved over hers with a sweetness that made her knees weak. It was a kiss her tired soul could melt into. A soul that had found its mate…

EPILOGUE

THEY wandered through the park. An orchestra was playing 'How Deep is Your Love' in the distance, the sun was shining and Rick's arm was around Tara's waist.

Rick steered her under a flowering jacaranda tree where a picnic rug was laid out on the grass.

Tara couldn't help but smile. It was set for two, a rose lying across one of the plates. 'Rick?'

'You must hear a lot of proposals,' he murmured softly.

Her stomach fluttered. 'Yes,' she said tentatively. 'A few, I guess.' With some clients she couldn't seem to avoid them.

'Care to hear one more?'

She shot him a wide-eyed look. He couldn't be serious? 'From you?' she asked, smiling.

He dropped to his knee. 'Tara, you wouldn't believe how much my life has changed since I met you.'

'I can guess.' She grinned. He was obviously pulling her leg...

'My life was dull without your smile, without your touch, without your sweet voice saying my name.'

She laughed. 'This sounds familiar.'

'Excuse me. Can I just do this without comments?' he said quite seriously.

Tara's heart lurched, her senses swirling in excitement. 'Sure.'

'I love you with all my heart and soul, Tara Andrews. I want to share my life with you. Please…complete me.'

'And?'

He let out a sigh. 'Will you do me the honour of becoming my wife?'

She pursed her lips. Oh, my. Oh, wow. Oh, Jeez. 'Maybe,' she said, trying to stay calm.

Rick's eyes were wide. 'What?'

She couldn't help but laugh. 'Yes. Of course.' She dropped into his arms and hugged him tightly to her. 'Absolutely, totally, positively, thoroughly, yes!'

He pulled back, flicking open a little red velvet heart-shaped box. The three-carat, marquise-cut rose diamond in the middle glittered in the afternoon sun. The two pearl-shaped diamonds on either side made the amazing ring absolutely incredible, and perfect.

'Oh, my—'

Rick took the ring from the box and slid it on to her finger, staring up into her eyes with all the love in his heart.

Tara's heart contracted and her eyes burned. 'Oh, Rick.' She wrapped her arms around him and kissed him, her pulse racing. 'I love you.'

'So, are you going to give me a score for my proposal?' he asked between kisses.

Tara looked him in the face, sobering. 'It was the…
the best proposal I've ever heard.'

'Really?' Rick's eyes glittered.

'Because it was mine.' She smiled warmly at the man
she loved. And she loved him so very much. 'And from
you.'

'Nice afterthought.' Rick pulled her down on to the
grass beside the rug, wrapping her in his warm, strong
arms.

'I thought so.' Tara couldn't help but smile as she
looked up into Rick's face. All she needed now was a
big white wedding with all the trimmings, even better
than Jack and Kasey's, that could showcase *all* of
Camelot's talents, to splash through the papers, and
she'd have everything.

She flicked the buttons on Rick's shirt, slipping her
hand against his warm flesh. 'Could you do *me* a favour?'

'Anything,' he said, his voice smooth and deep.

She ran her hand down his ribs, gazing into his eyes.
'Love me.'

Rick brushed his lips over hers. 'Forever and always.'

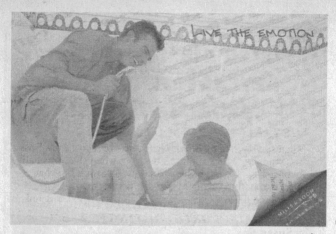

Modern Romance™
...international affairs
– seduction and
passion guaranteed

Medical Romance™
...pulse-raising
romance – heart-
racing medical drama

Tender Romance™
...sparkling, emotional,
feel-good romance

Sensual Romance™
...teasing, tempting,
provocatively playful

Historical Romance™
...rich, vivid and
passionate

Blaze Romance™
...scorching hot
sexy reads

27 new titles every month.

Live the emotion

MILLS & BOON®

MB4

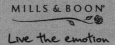

MILLS & BOON®

Live the emotion

Tender Romance™

THE TAKEOVER BID by Leigh Michaels (9 to 5)

When sexy Wyatt Reynolds claims he's Melanie's new boss
she's stunned. How can he be her boss when she owns half
the business? He might be absolutely gorgeous, but that
doesn't stop him driving Mel mad. Wyatt seems
determined to take over – with Mel as part of the bargain!

A MARRIAGE WORTH WAITING FOR
by Susan Fox

When Selena Keith is injured in a car crash, Morgan
Conroe demands she move into his home. Selena's
shocked, she hasn't seen Morgan for two long years, though
her love for him still burns strong. But Morgan has realised
what he let go before – and he's not letting her go again...

THE PREGNANT TYCOON by Caroline Anderson

Rich and successful, Izzy Brooke has everything – except
love. Then she's reunited with Will Thompson, the
boyfriend she had as a teenager, and soon finds she's
unexpectedly pregnant! This is the life-change she wants –
but there are secrets about Will's past which they must
confront before they can embrace the future...

THE HONEYMOON PROPOSAL
by Hannah Bernard

Joanna has dreamed of marrying Matt from the day they
first kissed – their wedding day, which should have been the
happiest day of her life. But the relationship is a sham and
the marriage is a fake. So, if it's all pretence, why does it
feel so heart-stoppingly real? And why has Matt proposed a
very *real* honeymoon?

On sale 7th May 2004

*Available at most branches of WHSmith, Tesco, Martins, Borders,
Eason, Sainsbury's and all good paperback bookshops.*

0404/02

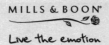

MILLS & BOON®

Live the emotion

PENNINGTON

BOOK ELEVEN

Available from 7th May 2004

*Available at most branches of WHSmith, Tesco, Martins, Borders,
Eason, Sainsbury's and most good paperback bookshops.*

PENN/RTL/11

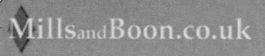